Vyse Av

MW00953401

VYSE AVENUE

Charles H. Freundlich

Also by Charles H. Freundlich

PERETZ SMOLENSKIN: His Life and Thought

VYSE AVENUE

A NOVEL

By

CHARLES H. FREUNDLICH

Charles H. Freundlich

VYSE AVENUE

Copyright 2013 by Charles H. Freundlich

ISBN -13: 978-1484807149
ISBN -10: 1484807146

DEDICATION

To

DEBORAH

*My dear wife, partner, soul mate, best friend,
and Star*

Charles H. Freundlich

Vyse Avenue

CONTENTS

PREFACE   9

LADY IN THE WINDOW   17

BRONX RHAPSODY   35

BREINA   49

THE PENITENT   67

THE GREMLINS   85

SOL'S JOURNEY   95

MARVIN   115

SEYMOUR   125

PARADISE GAINED   135

ELAINE   151

CONFRONTATIONS   167

NEW HORIZONS   179

HOMECOMING   195

FRAGMENTS   217

INGATHERING   233

ABOUT THE AUTHOR   251

Charles H. Freundlich

PREFACE

WHEN I MOVED to New England, people were surprised to learn that I came from the Bronx and they would ask, "Isn't that the home of the New York Yankees?" Or they would exclaim, "I understand your Zoo is the second largest in the world, and your Botanical Gardens are peerless."

People often think that New York is synonymous with Manhattan or Brooklyn and that The Bronx is a minor part of the greatest city. Let me relate a number of facts about

Charles H. Freundlich

The Bronx and its outstanding personalities that dispel this erroneous notion. Here are some of the Bronx-born celebrities in the American Pantheon: Hank Greenberg, of the Detroit Tigers, the greatest slugger of his generation, grew up in the Bronx on North Crotona Park Avenue and led the James Monroe High School baseball team to the city championship. Yes, it's true the first Jewish super athlete refused to play on Yom Kippur in 1934, while the Tigers were pursuing a long-awaited pennant, much to the displeasure of the fans. In addition, Greenberg was the highest paid player, the first to top $100,000.

Only recently, the world of music lamented the loss of two renowned Bronx-born singers. The internationally acclaimed soprano, Regina Resnik (another alumnus of James Monroe High School), who performed more than 300 times at the New York Metropolitan Opera, and the celebrated star of pop music, Eydie Gorme (a graduate of Taft High School), who sang with her equally-talented husband, Steve Lawrence. Her classmate was the famous film director, Stanley Kubrick. Another alumnus of Monroe High School, Jules Pfeiffer, became a celebrated cartoonist and won the Pulitzer Prize in Journalism.

Herman Wouk was another Pulitzer Prize winner, who achieved fame for "The Caine Mutiny." Wouk had previously authored "City Boy: The Adventures of Herbie Bookbinder," a delightful novel about life in the Bronx prior to the Great Depression, which became an international favorite and a classic.

The list of prestigious authors includes the poet and storyteller, Edgar Allen Poe, master of mystery, who spent his final years in the Bronx. His home ensconced in Poe

Park, has become a shrine for the literati. Sholom Aleichem, the most universally loved Yiddish author, spent his last years on Kelly Street, a few blocks from my home on Vyse Avenue; and 100,000 people attended his funeral in 1916. Other esteemed Yiddish writers were: Joseph Opatashu and Chaim Grade - generally considered the greatest poet and novelist of our era.

Kelly Street, incidentally, was also the home of Colin Powell, former Secretary of State and Chairman of The Joint Chiefs of Staff of the U.S. Military Forces. He attended P.S. 20 near Simpson Street - later called *Fort Apache.* He graduated from Morris High School as did the famous alumni: Milton Berle, first King of T.V. comedy, Jules Dassin, film director of "Never On Sunday," and Abe Burrows, author of "Guys and Dolls." Another iconic author is Cynthia Ozick, who grew up in the Pelham Bay section, where her parents owned a drug store.

Nobel Laureate, Dr. Jonas Salk, the discoverer of a Polio vaccine, lived on Elsmere Place near Crotona Park. Let us not forget Melvin Schwartz, a graduate of Bronx High School of Science (many claim it is the best in the world), who won the Nobel Prize in Physics in 1988. Geraldine Ferraro, the first woman to run for national office, grew up on Longfellow Avenue.

Among the many celebrated entertainers were: comedian, Robert Klein, who wrote most humorously about his growing up on Decatur Avenue; Jan Murray (Murray Janofsky) who hosted the #1 daytime show on T.V., "Treasure Hunt;" Red Buttons (Aaron Chwiatt), who also lived on Tremont Avenue; Judd Hirsch, who was successful both on Broadway and in Hollywood, who grew up in the

11

Claremont section; and Regis Philbin, host of a popular daily morning show, who grew up on Cruger Avenue in the Pelham Parkway section, where he recalled playing Stickball.

Who can forget the now classic lines, "I love you Spartacus," by Tony Curtis (Bernard Herschel Schwartz), with his distinct Bronx accent, in the 1960 film by Stanley Kubrick? Hollywood came to the Bronx with the Martin Scorsese film, "Raging Bull" (1980), about the life of the Bronx-born boxer, Jake LaMotta. Robert DeNiro won an Academy Award for the starring role; and he also appeared in another cinematic epic, "A Bronx Tale."

"Marty," the 1955 Academy Award winning film, written by Paddy Chayefsky, was screened in the Arthur Avenue Market, an Italian enclave. This film established the reputation of Ernest Borgnine, playing a soft-hearted butcher who was single, who found his sweetheart at the "Starlight Ballroom," adjacent to the RKO Chester Cinema. Borgnine also starred with Bette Davis in the film, "The Catered Affair" (1956), also written by Chayefsky, about the frustration of a taxi driver trying to schedule a wedding for his daughter at the exclusive Bronx Concourse Plaza Hotel. This luxurious hotel on the Grand Concourse also served as the main speaker's venue for Presidents: Truman, Eisenhower and Kennedy, and also for the Yankee Baseball stars.

Prominent leaders in the world of finance included: Armand Hammer, the internationally renowned industrialist, and Lloyd Blankfein, the postal worker's son, who became the CEO and head of Goldman Sachs - one of most successful investment institutions in the world. The U.S.Holocaust Museum in Washington, one of the most frequently visited tourist attractions, was made possible, largely, through the leadership of a housing and mall developer by the name of Albert Abramson.

Though the smallest of New York's five boroughs, The Bronx - with its forty-three square miles - is as large as Paris. It has more than one million and four hundred thousand residents, and by 1940, forty-nine percent were Jewish - making it the most densely populated Jewish community in the world, and with abundant Yiddish speakers. It is the only borough on the mainland of the U.S.A. It inspired master-builder, Robert Moses, to erect three magnificent bridges: *The Whitestone*, *Throgs Neck* and *Triborough*, which connected the Bronx to Manhattan (Island) and Queens (Long Island). Robert Moses was responsible for planning the six-mile Cross Bronx Expressway at a cost of forty-seven million dollars, the most expensive road ever built. It decimated whole neighborhoods, hundreds of apartment buildings, and uprooted thousands (mostly poorer people), in order to accelerate the travel between the Bronx and Queens. This mostly disruptive thruway, completed in 1963 - accommodating 145,000 vehicles daily - was a mixed blessing; it created the need for new public housing in the Bronx.

Freedomland was reputed to be the largest entertainment center in the world. It was built on landfill and swamp land in the Pelham Bay area of the Bronx in 1960. A larger version of Disneyland, it embraced 85 acres and could accommodate 90,000 customers daily with its wide assortment of games and programs. At a cost of 65 million dollars, it often attracted 72,000 cars daily, but was not profitable. At the end of the first year, it had lost 8 million dollars; and in 1964, it was sold to the Co-op City Development. The failure was attributed to the forthcoming competition of the World's Fair in New York in 1964 (another Robert Moses project), while others argued that the sale was to make a profit.

The Co-op City Development built between 1966 and 1968, on the same locale, became one of the wonders of the world - the largest housing project ever built. With 35 high-rise apartments, 15,372 units and 55,000 people, it became the tenth largest city in the United States. Among its prestigious tenants were Congressman Elliot L. Engel, actress, Queen Latifah, serial killer, David Berkowitz (son of Sam), and most notable, Sonia Sotomayor, the first Hispanic Associate Justice of the U.S. Supreme Court.

Apartment buildings abounded in The Bronx topography. They were mostly six floors, lacking elevators and occupied by Italian, Jewish and Irish immigrants. When the radio networks began to feature a family program of immigrant life, *The Goldbergs,* their choice, was the fictitious address, 1038 East Tremont Avenue in the East Bronx, a main thoroughfare for shopping and cinema. The show began in 1929, during the Great Depression, and the lovable and wise Jewish mother, Molly Goldberg, captured the hearts of all America.

The show continued into the age of television and was popular until 1956. Gertrude Berg, the creator, writer and star, was second only to Eleanor Roosevelt as the country's outstanding woman - but she was number one as the highest paid woman, earning $100,000. "Yoo hoo, Mrs. Goldberg," became the most recognized sound in radio, reflecting the saga of the immigrant experience. Molly's

Vyse Avenue

Yiddish-English (part of her role) and warm persona rendered the Jewish immigrant an authentic branch of Americana.

In the course of years, the stately apartment buildings have vanished, deracinated and ravaged by drug addicts and unscrupulous landlords. Morris High School and James Monroe High School, which were the crucibles and training grounds for tens of thousands of upward mobile Bronx youth, are gone. Their impressive buildings were demolished or converted into alternate educational sites. The closing of Alexander's department store, where one could shop leisurely for bargains, was woeful. The transforming of the opulent and palatial Loew's Paradise into a multiplex was a grievous loss. Gone was its ceiling of simulated stars, and luxuriant decor which compared well with the any Opera House. This Saturday night destination was both a romantic and enchanting experience for countless young lovers.

The south end of the Grand Concourse housed the Courthouse and the prestigious Concourse Plaza Hotel - the Bronx equivalent of the Waldorf Astoria, which has been restructured into condominiums. "The Boulevard" is only a shadow of its luminescence; and its three cinemas have been replaced with bargain stores. Gone, are the prestigious Synagogues on North Crotona Park, Kelly Street, Hunts Point, Bryant Avenue, Minford Place and the Grand Concourse. They endure as churches serving the general community.

The greatest loss is the community; the exodus of thousands of immigrants - Italian, Jewish, Polish and Irish - who created a colorful tapestry of the American dream. Hard-working, devoted, and loyal to their families, they raised themselves and their children to aspire and strive for a better life - because they believed in the American dream. They loved America and were proud when their sons went off to war.

The original immigrants have been replaced by other ethnic groups. Would anyone remember the Stickball teams, the *Robins* and the *Gremlins*, the corner grocery, the candy store, the beautiful cinemas, the small, store-front *shuls*, called *shtiebels* and the art-deco apartment buildings on the Grand Concourse? The kids on the block, with their peculiar nicknames: *Bones, Screw, Schnitz, Red, Moe, Duke, Mutsey, Heshy, Doc, Buddy and Coke* – have vanished.

"VYSE AVENUE," is a work of fiction. It attempts to portray the saga of one Jewish family and a community, prevailing over poverty - during the Great Depression, World War II, and the renascence of Israel

I AM MOST GRATEFUL TO DEBBY, my wife and partner, whose invaluable advice and criticism enabled me to complete this novel. Special thanks: to my older brother, Murray (Moish), who provided much important information and details of life in the Bronx; to my younger brother, Chester, who recounted many of his interesting memories about the cultural and social life of the neighborhood; and to Charles Rube whose technical advice was terrific.

Charles H. Freundlich   Boca Raton, Florida
July 20, 2013   Shabbat Nachamu 5773

THE LADY IN THE WINDOW

PEOPLE THOUGHT it very bizarre to see that lady in the window. Why she was there and what was she looking for? As people on the block passed by, they would greet her and often stayed to chat. Gittel Friedman was cordial, garrulous and had become an institution on Vyse Avenue. From her ground floor bedroom window, hardly five feet above the sidewalk, she looked like a sphinx. Her corpulent arms beneath her breasts, she leaned on a pillow on the window sill, looking out and greeting everyone.

17

She smiled affectionately when she spied Jenny Moskowitz who lived on the third floor, "Did you hear that the landlord was going to cut down on the heat this winter or else give us a raise?"

"It never will happen. We are paying too much as it is now," Jenny replied.

"But what happens if she does cut down on the heat?"

"So we'll freeze to death."

"Leave it to our landlord, Mrs. Levine - she should be well and not have a heart attack. Did you see the tomatoes on Jennings Street? Ten cents a pound, a plague on them! Tell me, how is your husband, Benny feeling? I heard he had an operation."

"What operation - a small procedure to correct his hernia. He's doing fine."

"What about Mr. O'Neil from the fourth floor? I heard he was hurt lifting a large sack of potatoes. They think it was a heart attack."

"No big deal, maybe a strained shoulder muscle."

"And how is your family?" Jenny asked.

"Thank God. My boys, Seymour and Marvin, write from Korea that they are coming home soon. Sol is in Israel studying in a yeshiva. He will be receiving his ordination soon. Elaine calls me every day from Jersey. She has two beautiful boys. No evil eye on my grandchildren."

"You're lucky Gittel. My Benny, may he be well, does not work regularly. If it's not a Hernia - then it's Asthma; he's a heavy smoker."

"We all have our little packs to carry. But let's talk about nice things. I've cooked a large pot of chicken soup with noodles, carrots and onions - too much for Louis and me. Would you like some?"

"That's kind of you. I like you, Gittel; and I like your cooking. I'll be glad to have some. I know Benny will love it."

Gittel felt passionate about cooking and spent half the day in the kitchen. But she was lonely for her children and reached out to the neighbors to find meaning and purpose. Once, looking out the window she saw some boys fighting down the block. Irving, a little boy, was on the floor being kicked by a bunch of kids from Hoe Avenue. Gittel took her dish towel and ran down the street screaming and waving her towel, driving the older boys away. She spat at one of the Hoe Avenue bunch and threatened him with her towel. "A stroke you should have," she shouted and picked up the small boy. She brought him to her apartment and washed his face which was drenched with tears and dirt. Gittel was the guardian of Vyse Avenue.

Conversation by Gittel's window was always light, but often lengthy. People knew that they could talk and Gittel would listen. One wag suggested that she was waiting for the Messiah. Others suspected that Gittel was a born *yenta,* and had nothing better to do than waste her time prying into other people's personal affairs. Their suspicions were erroneous.

GITTEL'S LOOKING out the window reflected a deep-felt, longing. She was hoping and praying that one day walking down Vyse Avenue, she would see her father, Avram Abba, walking side-by-side with his second wife and greeting her.

19

She had last received an international post card from her father in Galicia (now occupied by the USSR and part of Ukraine), in February of 1941. The post card indicated that the family was well-treated under the new regime. But she knew that her father, a merchant, would have his business confiscated by the Communist regime. Perhaps he would be imprisoned, or sent to Siberia. By June 22, 1941, the Nazis had invaded the Russian-occupied portion of Poland, formerly Galicia, and initiated the genocide that would take the lives of 800,000 Jews in the area. Polish Jews who had fled to the Russian occupied zone were deported to Siberia, but they survived the Nazi slaughtering. Was her father one of the lucky few? The inquiries with the *Joint* proved futile. The swift massacres of Jews in the area by the *SS Einzatgruppen* and the Ukrainians, left few survivors to tell of the horrors or have knowledge of any other survivors.

GITTEL WAS REFLECTING about her first encounter with the Ukrainian soldiers in 1918. She was sixteen when the Austrian armies retreated from their territories in Galicia; and the area became the battleground between the invading Polish armies and the newly formed Ukrainian militias under Simeon Petlura. The retreat of the Austrian military created a state of anarchy; the rabble began looting the Jewish homes, raping the women and beating the men.

Gittel was hidden in the attic of one of the homes which Huna, her grandfather, rented to a friendly Ukrainian. For weeks, the *pogroms* continued unabated until the Polish army restored a measure of public order. But the Ukrainian militias counter-attacked and public order gave way to more looting and mayhem. After three weeks of hiding, the Ukrainian mob broke through the doors where Gittel and her family were hidden.

Huna Rudnick was dragged into the street amid shouts, "Jew where is your money hidden?" Huna pleaded with them, "I will give you all my money. But please do not harm my family." The soldiers laughed and then agreed. Huna led the soldiers to the edge of the Jewish cemetery, where he had buried a wooden box with the family jewelry and silver ornaments. "Take it and leave us alone." The soldiers were pleased to receive the Jew's treasure.

"Jew, you must have more zlotys hidden."

They began beating him when Gittel ran to them screaming, "*Vilde chayos* [wild animals] - leave my *zeide* alone!"

She threw herself on the man beating her grandfather; and began pounding him with her fists with all her might. But this effort only provoked raucous laughter and amusement.

"And where is your Daddy?"

Avram Abba approached the soldiers nervously and lifted his father from the ground.

"Now let us see how the Jews, who cannot fight like men, can dance like bears."

The soldiers formed a circle and began singing and clapping their hands while Huna and Avram Abba began dancing and hopping." They were ecstatic, gloating over the sight of terrified Jews dancing like bears.

Gittel never forgot the sight of her grandfather's bloodied face and his torn, muddy caftan. She thought, "How could God have allowed these wild savages to degrade her esteemed grandfather, the renowned elder of the *shtetl*?"

GITTEL FELT IT HER DUTY to preserve and honor the memory of her family and reclaim the long lost pedigree of her youth. It was a matter of pride. She would recall vividly this special *yichus* [ancestry], when she felt the weight of her poverty and her loss of status in America. Some *Goldene Medina*!

She was the first grandchild of the notable Huna Rudnick, a wealthy landlord, and a "privileged Jew" in the Empire of Franz Josef. Gittel was the object of Huna's strong affections and was given private tutoring in Hebrew, when she was six. By the time she was seven, she was adept in reading and writing and had begun the study of *Humash*.

Her father, Avram Abba, assisted in the collecting of rent for the family's property and never had to work with his hands like the common people of the town of Hustechko. Gittel never ceased boasting to her poor cousins and to her *landsleit* [countrymen], "My father never worked."

THE FIRST WORLD WAR and the internecine conflicts and atrocities of the passing armies, had devastated the small towns in Galicia, where thousands of Jews were massacred, and the Rudnick's property was seized. Her town was now occupied by the "Jew-hating Poles," she lamented, and the family was destitute. Without money, Gittel would have no dowry to find a suitable husband. Her father decided that she, the oldest daughter, must go to America; acquire a dowry to attain a husband, and send back some money to assist her family.

Vyse Avenue

GITTEL RUDNICK was eighteen, slightly buxom, with dark eyes, when she arrived in New York City, after a two-week voyage in steerage. She was greeted by her Aunt Clara, who had settled five years earlier, and established a small shop on Orchard Street on the Lower East Side of Manhattan. She would work in her aunt's shop; receive room and board, and five dollars a week. The clamor of the street, busy shops, men hawking their wares, and the crowded conditions of the tenements, were slightly mitigated by the fact that she was one of thousands of *Greeners*, new immigrants, who shared her ordeal and spoke her language.

Aunt Clara delineated Gittel's responsibilities in the shop in Yiddish with a few chosen English words: "First thing in the morning, you must sweep the sidewalk in front of the shop, so that people will want to enter a fine establishment. After your morning tea and roll, you will help sort out the various hats and gloves according to size. We eat at twelve noon, and you will help prepare the soup and noodles and wash the dishes. Do you understand that I am paying you an excellent salary for a *Greener* who just arrived?"

Gittel thought, "I am a servant. In my father's house we had servants to clean and prepare our meals." She quickly disabused herself that she was a guest, a person of stature, the first grandchild of Huna Rudnick.

Three months later, she received a letter from her father.

TO MY DEAR AND PRECIOUS DAUGHTER GITTELE, LONG MAY YOU LIVE,

First, I send you the best wishes of your dear grandfather Huna, God protect him, and those of your mother, for your good health and prosperity in America. Also, send our greetings to your dear Tante Clara, may God keep her in good health, and be doubly blessed for providing you with room and board and a good job.

Second, we thank God for His blessings following the war and enabling us to stay in our home though many *landsleit* have fled to Germany and America.

Third, we are starving! There is little work, and we have no wood to heat our home during this cold winter. Our clothes are like those of a pauper and your grandfather is ashamed to attend synagogue with his rags. He is deeply depressed and wishes every day that God would bring him to eternal rest. We look forward to receiving your monthly four dollars which you promised us in your last letter. Have you contacted Rabbi Perlman to help us? If you could provide us with two ship tickets, hardly more than two hundred dollars, we could join you. Then, we could bring over the rest of the family. Perhaps Tante Clara, or Rabbi Perlman, could fill out the proper papers.

Love and blessings,
Your father, Avram Abba

The Rav of the town, Yankel Perlman, a highly-respected Talmudist, had come to New York with his children immediately after the war and was appointed to a prominent *shul* on the Lower East Side. Could he prepare the necessary papers for the remaining members of Gittel's family? After all, where did Rav Perlman and his family find safety when the invading armies of Poland crossed through

Galicia, demolishing homes and inflicting death and mayhem on women and children? Was it not in the home of Huna Rudnick, a privileged Jew of Austria? But Rabbi Perlman was struggling to establish himself and was unable to assist in preparing the affidavits for Gittel's father.

Gittel worked long hours, six days a week, in her aunt's shop and sent home four dollars a month. The letters continued to flow from her father unabated with its vivid description of their desperate ordeal to survive. Gittel realized that she was unable to rescue her parents, her younger brothers and sisters, and focused on her own survival. After a while, the pleading letters from her father ceased.

Avram Abba was able to establish himself as a merchant of fabrics imported from Lemberg, now called Lvov, with the help of a loan from his uncle, who lived there. He wrote to Gittel and Rav Perlman more encouraging letters about the Pilsudski regime, which was friendly to Jews and businessmen, and kept those "extremist anti-Semitic Poles" in their place. But he was, nevertheless, desirous to leave Poland and come to America, to join the many *landsleit* of Hustechko who had emigrated after the war.

Six months later, another letter arrived.

DEAR GITTELE, MAY GOD KEEP YOU IN GOOD HEALTH,

First, let me send you our best wishes for the coming New Year. We pray that you will soon find your *bashert* [destined person], whom God has allotted to you, to marry and raise a Jewish family. Amen.

Next, let me ask you again to help us come to America, your mother and I and your brothers and sisters. Your dear grandfather, Huna, long may he live, is depressed and weeps all day. He does not wish to abandon our beloved Hustechko and the cemetery with graves of five generations of the Rudnick family. But there is no future for us here and we must come to America. The cost of a ship ticket is a little more than $100.00 for each of us and you will have to fill out the proper documentation, and affidavits in New York. I know that Rabbi Perlman, and his son, who speaks English, can help out. Remember how we saved his family during the war? We look forward to your letters and your four dollars each month.

> Love and best wishes to your Tante Clara and uncle
> Your father, Avram Abba

Gittel felt dispirited over her inability to rescue her family. Little did they know that her weekly salary of five dollars from her aunt, and the monthly check she sent home, left little money to purchase ship tickets to America. In addition, she had to save money for her own future. Her visits to Rabbi Perlman were fruitless. He had neither the money, nor the political connections to provide affidavits for her family.

After six years, Gittel had accumulated the sum of two hundred dollars, a worthy dowry, and began to seek a husband. Could she marry without her father's approval of the groom? What would people say? No respectable woman married without the presence of family. She could not prepare either the necessary documentation or send a ship ticket for her father to come to America. This distressed her, but she was struggling to survive and make her own way. She barely spoke English and was fortunate that most of her customers spoke Yiddish.

Gittel was committed to the idea that a woman was not complete, not blessed, unless she had a husband and children. Women who had to work in shops and factories were disgraceful slaves, oppressed by harsh and cruel bosses, who would not only exploit their labor, but often abuse them sexually. Marriage was the key to a woman's liberation. She would be protected by her husband and could earn extra money, if needed, by working at home. It was most undignified for a woman to work in the labor market - a reflection that her husband was a *schlemiel,* a loser, who could not support her.

Gittel sought the services of a *shadchan*, a marriage broker, Mr. S. Fischoff, who advertised in the Yiddish *Daily Forward*. For a modest fee of ten dollars, he assured Gittel he would arrange the *perfect match made in Heaven*. When he came to Aunt Clara's shop, Gittel beheld an undistinguished man. Mr. S. Fischoff was slightly hunched with a greyish goatee, a dark fedora, rumpled suit, and a pair of scuffed shoes that needed the services of a shoemaker. His deeply-lined and unshaven face did little to add to his distinction.

Gittel pleaded, "My future husband should come from a fine family, like my own, from Galicia - no Russian or Romanian, please. And he should be educated with knowledge of German and a graduate of gymnasia. He should *daven* every morning and put on *tefillin* like my father - but no beard or *payos.* He should speak English, even with an accent. Most important he should make a living and want children."

27

The first match presented was Zalman Klepfish, a short, corpulent man, in his mid-thirties, from Kiev. When he was seated in Aunt Clara's living room, he asked for an ash tray and lit up a cigarette.

"What is your line of work," Aunt Clara asked.

"Well, I have been trained as a diamond cutter in Russia, but since coming to America I have had to make adjustments in my profession."

"And what is your present profession?"

"Well, for the time being, I am a kitchen helper in Kass' Restaurant. You know the famous restaurant on Delancey Street."

"You mean you are a dishwasher?"

"Only - temporary."

Gittel interjected, "You look like an honest man, Mr. Klepfish, and you will find your *bashert*. But I don't think you are for me."

The second candidate was Shloimie Fenster, a widower in his forties, with three children.

Gittel cried to the matchmaker, "I deserve someone better."

"Better?" questioned Mr. Fischoff. "Dear Gittel, you are a fine young lady, but you have no family here in America. What kind of wedding could you provide? Your dowry is very modest. You cannot be choosy."

Gittel was determined to marry someone suitable for her class - someone she could love her and make her family proud.

The next candidate was a working man, good-looking and religious. When he began speaking to her she realized that he was a Litvak. "My family never married with Litvaks," she complained to Mr. Fischoff.

The next candidate was Berel Schwartz, a tall handsome man, finely-tailored, with a flower in his lapel. Gittel greeted him with a broad smile. She was ecstatic over Berel's refinement and elegant manner. Having been seated, Mr. Schwartz declared, "Let us get to the bottom line. How large is the dowry?" Gittel was speechless and left the room crying, "The pig isn't interested in me."

Finally, the perfect match arrived. It was Louis Friedman, slim with wavy, blond hair, blue eyes, ruddy complexion and smooth skin that belied his thirty-two years, (most of which he spent as a factotum in various restaurants). He was religious, prayed every morning with *tallis* and *tefillin* and spoke Low German in addition to Yiddish.

His accented English was superior to Gittel's. However, he had not attended gymnasia and had no formal education beyond the age of twelve. He had mastered *Humash with Rashi* in *heder* as a child and could rattle off the Hebrew prayers with great aplomb. He was neatly dressed and diffident. He was the son of the late Moshe Yosef Friedman from Bukovina, then part of Galicia in the Austria-Hungary Empire of Franz Josef, now part of Romania, and whose family was devoted to the Sadegera Rebbe. Moshe Yosef Friedman had come to America before the war with his daughter, Miriam, and his two sons, Nuta and Louis, lest they be drafted into the Austrian army. Miriam, his older sister doted on Louis like a helpless child.

In contrast, Gittel had come to America without family and quickly assimilated into the inhospitable reality of urban life. She, unlike Louis, was buxom, with broad shoulders, already twenty-four, considered old, and was desperate to marry. When Gittel met Louis she was somewhat disappointed. Her family, the Rudnicks, had all been corpulent, a sign of prosperity, with dark hair and brown eyes. Louis was slight of build and very blond, almost Nordic. As they sat together in Aunt Clara's parlor, Gittel was apprehensive. What should she ask him? She had never been socially involved with a man.

"Do you like honey cake?" she asked Louis.

"I love honey cake. I also love *mandelbroit*, nut loaf, Louis responded.

"I can bake and will keep a kosher home and light candles every Sabbath eve," Gittel responded.

"I have a steady job working in my brother's fruit shop."

"So, you are a businessman? My family has always been in business. My grandfather, Huna was a landlord, a privileged Jew in Hustechko, and my father never worked with his hands."

Louis countered, "My family had a large mill in Bukovina before the war. We left in 1912 just before the war broke out. We had to abandon our property to save ourselves. My older brother, Shmuel, remained in Lemberg and did very well as a manufacturer of uniforms for the army. Unfortunately, he knew no Polish when Lemberg became Lvov and was suspected of being a spy. The Poles shot him."

A moment of silence….

"My older brother, Moshe, served with honor in the Austrian army. He died in Budapest in 1917 during the Flu epidemic," Gittel replied.

Gittel was delighted to know that Louis' family was "better class," not common people, who worked with their hands.

"I would like to open my own grocery store. I know the food business very well," Louis continued.

"I, too, have been in business working with my aunt the past six years. She sells women's clothes, socks, shoes and hats."

"Do you think you could work twelve hours a day, six days a week in a grocery store?" Louis questioned.

Gittel was not surprised by the question; and she realized that Louis would not support her. This was America, she mused, and women were expected to work with their husbands in their shops.

"I am strong and healthy. I will work with my husband twenty-four hours a day. With my dowry, we will be able to open our own store. We can live in the back of the store until we have children and save enough money for our own apartment."

Aunt Clara interrupted the conversation, "Enough talk for today. Louis, come for dinner next Friday evening, with your sister, Miriam. Then, we can make plans."

What had to be discussed between Gittel and Louis? Gittel knew that she was expected to get married, keep a Kosher home and beget children. As a proper Jewish woman, she would be deferential to her husband, even if she were wiser. Louis knew what was expected of him: to support and honor his wife, produce children and perform the commandments of the Torah. They could not fathom the modern ideas of romance and happiness. Life was harsh and based on duty and responsibility to family, Israel and God.

Did he have to love this strange woman he hardly knew? He had been advised by his sister, Miriam; that love would come naturally *after* marriage. Miriam, who was married and experienced, would advise him whether Gittel was his designated soul mate from Heaven, and she would also take charge of the wedding arrangements.

Nuta came to Miriam's apartment that evening and the discussion concentrated on the prospective bride for their younger and ingenuous brother.

"What was your impression? Nuta asked.

"She's perfect for Louis. She has experience in business, a good brain, looks strong, and can take care of Louis. Most important, she comes from a good religious family like ours, and will make him happy. She's a nice looking, dark-haired woman - no beauty, but okay. She's twenty-four and is willing to work hard. She's not one of those wild, radical communists you meet on the East Side."

"What about a dowry?" Nuta asked.

"She has a few hundred dollars - enough to start a small business, maybe a grocery shop. Maybe her aunt will also help out."

"If only Papa could have lived to see the wedding," Nuta reflected.

"I'll be going with Louis this Friday night to discuss the wedding plans with her Aunt Clara."

"I forgot. What is the bride's name?"

"Gittel Rudnick from Hustechko but she was given the name, *Gertrude,* on Ellis Island."

Gittel was relieved that Louis would marry her - a woman without the presence of her family. But with her dowry, they could open a small grocery store in the Bronx and plan a family.

The parties were agreeable. A month later, a modest wedding ceremony was performed by Rabbi Perlman, in his Chapel, without remuneration. It was followed by a festive dinner at the Little Hungary Restaurant, a few blocks away.

The party of sixteen wolfed down their chicken soup, stuffed cabbage, roast chicken and strudel. They then joined in an exultant dance around the newly-weds. Nuta offered the traditional *Seven Blessings* over a cup of wine, and Miriam presented the newly-weds with an envelope containing fifty dollars, a gift from her and her husband, John.

Between the dowry and the wedding gifts, Gittel found a modest one bedroom apartment with a toilet on the same floor. Gittel and *Leibel*, as she called Louis, moved into their newly rented apartment on Orchard Street and shared their first experience of love. Gittel did not return to her aunt's shop, though Louis would continue to work with his brother for the next seven months until they found a grocery store to buy in the Bronx, and live in the back.

Charles H. Freundlich

BRONX RHAPSODY

TIME PASSED quickly for Gittel and Louis in their new grocery store. It was obvious to Gittel that Louis was without business expertise and feckless. He found it difficult to make decisions regarding money and stock. The hours were long, starting at 6:00 A.M., and concluding at about 8:00 P.M. In addition, the physical labor was exhausting; Louis had to haul in the dairy products in heavy metal containers, and butter, in large vats. But Louis accepted the routine and did his work without complaint. He insisted that the heavy work was for a man and not for Gittel, who was already pregnant.

Customers sensed Louis's naiveté and exploited his weakness to bargain over the price for bread and milk. How could he, Louis thought, take money from a poor man who had to support his wife and little children? Sometimes, he cut a larger chunk of butter from the vat for a person that was dressed shabbily. He was a lame follower; and Gittel soon learned that she would be the dominant partner in their marriage. Louis was hard-working, kind and deferential to Gittel, who began to accept him as a junior partner in her life. As her pregnancy advanced, Gittel was given to emotional outbreaks. She criticized Louis' favors to poorer customers.

"We are running a business, not a charity," she shrieked. "You'll put us in the poor house."

The following year, Elaine was born; and Louis kissed her and played with her often, to the annoyance of Gittel. "Enough kissing and hugging," she scolded him. "There's work to do - you haven't swept up the front of the store."

Louis was oblivious as a stone to Gittel's nagging and scolding. The essential issue for him was food, security, and above all, the hope that the future would be brighter. Perhaps their small store would grow and be enlarged another fifteen feet from the side. Perhaps, they would enlarge the section for fresh produce. Most crucial, they would save enough to rent an apartment.

Gittel chafed at the heavy burden of her role as mother and grocer. She began putting on weight and her blood pressure increased. Her physician, Dr. Schatz, a graduate of the Vienna Medical School (but who was from Poland and spoke to her in Yiddish), admonished her that she had a dangerous sugar level. She had been stricken with diabetes. Thanks to Dr. Banting, who discovered insulin five years earlier, she would survive. She would have to be on a strict diet, reduce her weight, and avoid sweets. Gittel was nonplussed. The Rudnicks had all been corpulent, a sign of prosperity and status. Only the impoverished lacked a wide girth.

"How can I avoid eating honey cake, my favorite," she lamented."

"You want to die and leave me alone?" Louis rejoined.

Gittel would soon learn that life can continue without honey cake, without sweet Concord wine, and without the rich chocolate bars (that she nibbled on when there were no customers in sight). Each day became an ordeal, especially in the kitchen, where she was preparing dinner for Louis.

Miriam and Nuta, who lived in the neighborhood, came often on Friday afternoon to visit, make a few purchases, and offer emotional support. Gittel resented their overlong stays which took Louis away from his work.

"We will be renting an apartment next month, please God," Louis reported.

"Mazel Tov. How much is the rent?" Nuta asked.

"Twenty dollars a month and it has one bedroom and an eat-in kitchen," Louis smiled. "It's a palace with a large toilet and a shower in the bathtub," he continued.

Gittel added, "We ordered a beautiful bedroom set with a large chest of drawers. And we ordered a sofa and chairs and a large table for the living room which will also be our dining room. Our dreams have come true."

During the next three years, Gittel and Louis basked in the joy of their apartment which was large enough to accommodate their second child, Seymour.

One morning, when Louis opened the store at 6:00 A.M., a tall husky man pushed his way into the store and demanded money.

"Open the cash register now," he shouted waving a small pistol.

Louis quickly ran behind the counter but did not open the cash register.

Louis was overcome with fear and blurted, "Please mister, we need the money. Would you like some fresh rolls or some cupcakes?"

The man smashed Louis across the head with his pistol, opened the cash register, and lamented that there was hardly twenty dollars with change. Louis remained motionless on the floor while blood effused from his temple.

"You, son-of-a-bitch - where is the rest of the money? The thief shouted.

As Louis lay on the floor he cried, "We have no more; take some food and go, please."

The thief was infuriated and ran out of the store. Louis remained on the floor for a few minutes - too traumatized to get up. What would he say to Gittel? She would blame him for losing the day's cash reserve. Why didn't he resist and fight the thief? Louis had to think fast. He phoned his sister Miriam, "Hurry, come to the store - it's an emergency! Bring twenty dollars!"

Vyse Avenue

Louis had not washed the blood off his face when Miriam arrived. He explained what happened and Miriam thanked God that he was not killed. She kissed her younger brother and cautioned, "Next time, give the thief the money, foolish boy. Here's the twenty dollars." Miriam stanched the bleeding carefully and wrapped her handkerchief around his forehead.

When Gittel came to the front of the store with baby Seymour, later that morning, she beheld Louis with a blood-stained handkerchief around his head.

"A thief rushed in this morning when I opened the store, and demanded money from the cash register," Louis explained. "But I screamed, "Get the hell out you crook! He punched me and then I punched him back and threw him to the ground. Then I fell on the counter, after chasing him out of the store, and hurt my head. See, we have all the money in the cash register."

Gittel was grateful, "Blessed is God. You're okay. You saved the money! Are you sure you're not hurt Leibel?" From that time on, Gittel's respect and admiration for her Leibel increased. What would *she* have done if confronted by a thief? It was comforting to know that behind the quiet, passive façade, Leibel was tough and would protect his family.

The twenty dollars that covered the monthly rental of their store was significant for Gittel. The fear of being homeless was a constant source of anxiety which exacerbated her high blood pressure and increased her outbursts. She mused: to think that the granddaughter of Huna Rudnick, an esteemed landlord in Galicia, had to live in such a degrading state. Poverty, she recalled her grandfather telling her, was worse than death.

Settling in their new apartment, Gittel began looking out her window every afternoon when Seymour was asleep.

Within eight years, Gittel had four children. But the grocery failed; and they moved to Brooklyn, where they lived in a crowded one-bedroom apartment over a "taxpayer" for five years. Louis desperately sought work, even laborious, dirty temporary work.

Their fortunes changed when Miriam told them about the new apartments available in The Bronx, on Vyse Avenue, not far from her home. Miriam's husband, John, loaned the Friedmans one thousand dollars (not to be paid back) and they opened a commision bakery on Jennings Street. They shared a large space with a butcher store on the opposite side.

Their new four - room apartment in the East Bronx was an Elysium. The building was brick-red, six stories high and had a large atrium dividing the two wings. They were situated on the ground floor - no need for an elevator. There was a radiator in each room that provided ample steam heat and running hot water.

After a little more than a year, their bakery on Jennings Street failed. The children were deeply disappointed - Gittel would bring home Seven Layer and Checkerboard Chocolate cakes every evening.

Gittel felt desolate. She was frustrated with her daily life and remained contemptuous of her *landsleit,* parvenus, who thrived in America. She recalled the Schwartz family, common workers, tailors, who worshipped in the small *shul*, while her family, the Rudnicks, well-respected, was seated by the eastern wall of the Great Shul. But these nouveau riche had never invited her and Leibel to their home. They made their money in the *shmatteh* [garment] business. She comforted herself thinking - money alone, could not buy class, in the Old World - a theme which reverberated in her imagination.

The plight of Gittel's family worsened in 1939. The Russians invaded and occupied eastern Poland and the Post Cards from Gittel's father became laconic. What was happening to her world? As a child she thought of herself as an Austrian living in Galicia and recalled the blessed name of Franz Josef who had been good to her esteemed grandfather, Huna, and to all Jews. Her hometown had become Polish after the First World War and now it was Russian!

Following the Pearl Harbor attack, America increased its demand for airplanes, tanks, war-ships and steel. Louis found work in the Brooklyn Munitions factory and his generous salary paid the rent and enabled them to live in relative comfort.

Gittel continued to look out the window. She watched the passerbys and greeted them with a broad smile that invited conversation. The Italian women in the brownstones from across the street, were full-time homemakers, and had time to walk over and chat about their families and recipes for cakes. Their husbands worked long hours in construction, made an excellent living, and ate gargantuan dinners. Mr. Orzini had his own car, parked in front of the building, which was washed and shined every week. Afterwards, he would hose down the front sidewalk. The Italians, Gittel noted, knew how to maintain their property and stay in one place - not like the other immigrants who were like Gypsies - constantly moving.

When Gittel looked out her window she bewailed her happy childhood and the American dream that had not been hers. Perhaps her children would have a better life. Elaine was in high school and the three boys, Seymour, Sol and Marvin were succeeding in school. Perhaps, things would get better in Europe. Roosevelt would never allow Hitler to harm the Jews outside of Germany; her father and her brothers and sisters would be safe under Russian rule.

One morning, two well-dressed men knocked on the Friedman's apartment door. They were from the Brooklyn Munitions factory. There was an accident - a slight explosion. Louis had been hurt and was taken to the hospital. They offered their regrets and assured her that the Union would cover the hospital expenses. Their car was outside and they would bring her to the hospital. Gittel called on her friend, Mrs. Orzini to watch her apartment and to tell the children.

As they were approaching the hospital, Gittel realized, like an epiphany, that her Leibel was the most important person in her life. Their life together these past fourteen years were not without struggles and insecurity. They worked together and Leibel was loyal and dependable. Leibel's accident was a significant reality and she had to set aside her delusions of her past.

When she arrived at the hospital, Louis was asleep. The nurse told her that Louis had a severe concussion, but would survive. He needed rest for a few days and would return to work. Gittel held Leibel's hand and felt his warmth. She kissed him on the forehead and seated herself next to his bed. She called Miriam and Nuta; and they arrived within the hour. They sat for a while in the room speaking softly and then went to meet with the doctor. The report was optimistic. Leibel had regained consciousness. Gittel, Miriam and Nuta cried intensely together and praised God for Leibel's survival and healing.

"It was truly a miracle," Gittel said. "The worker next to Leibel was killed in the explosion."

Miriam cried, "We must give to t*zedakah* and then celebrate. When Leibel comes home, we'll have a beautiful dinner in my apartment on Sunday. Then we'll all go out to a movie on Southern Boulevard - agreed?" Gittel hugged Miriam and felt, for the first time, that she was also her sister. Nuta and his wife Zelda, Miriam and her husband, John became one family.

A year earlier, when Nuta was in need of an operation, he turned to Louis and Gittel for financial help. But they had little savings. Gittel said, "I can sell my diamond ring." But Zelda declined. They then turned to Miriam who asked her husband to help. John was expanding his fruit business and needed every dollar; but he agreed to pay the three hundred dollars to cover the hospital costs. Though John was an *outsider* - an Italian convert to Judaism- he became one of the family.

TWO WEEKS LATER, Gittel received a phone call.
"Hello. This is Blima."
"Blima - who?"
"Blima. You remember - when I was in your home in Hustechko."

Gittel was astounded. Could this be little Blima with whom she played in Hustechko, forty years earlier?

"This is Blima. I survived! I got your name from the *Joint*. I want to see you."

"Blima dear, please come. Do you have news about my father and family? Did they survive?"

"I will tell you everything when I visit."

Blima Lipschitz came with her husband, Ruven, also a Holocaust survivor, who limped.

After she was seated, Blima's woeful appearance told half the story. Her narrative was riveting and incisive.

"IT ALL BEGAN on June 22, 1941. I remember the exact date. For two years we were under the Russians. It was not good - but they protected us from the Nazis and the Ukrainians. Not all the Ukrainians were anti-Semites. In fact, one hid your father for more than a month. Your father's store was taken over by the Russians, but he was permitted to work there. Not bad at first - then the boss fired your father who was replaced by a Ukrainian.

"The first few days, the Nazis entered Hustechko and shot about 150 Jews who were gathered in the Chief Synagogue, where your family prayed. Then they passed new laws: no children in school, no doctors or lawyers allowed to practice, no Jew could shop at a store, and every Jew must wear a Star of David. But the worst came when they ordered all men between the ages of 14 to 60 to register for labor camp. But it was not for labor! As soon as they were eight kilometers outside Hustechko, they were all executed - after digging their own graves! And then, the Gestapo Chief, Doppler, ordered the *Judenrat*, which they had set up the prior day, to pay 1,000 Marks to pay for the bullets that were used to murder the Jews!"

44

Vyse Avenue

Gittel queried, "Blima, tell me about my father and mother."

"First, let me have a glass of water, please. Let me continue. All of your sisters and brothers had left Hustechko when the Russians came in 1939 and were sent to Siberia. They did not survive the terrible conditions of life there because they did not return after the war. Your father and mother were hidden by a Ukrainian peasant who was well-paid, for a full month. The first *Aktion* began on December 4, 1941 when more than three hundred Jews were assembled for inoculations for Typhus. But it was a lie! The people - men, women, and children, were locked in the Chief Synagogue, surrounded by the Nazis and Ukrainians, and kept there, without food and water, for two days!

"Then more than two thousand people were marched off to Siemakowcze, 12 kilometers away - forced to march in groups of five to the ravine, made to disrobe, and were executed with machine guns, while the Nazis and Ukrainians drank vodka and played music to cover the cries of the children. The clothes of the dead were sold, the following day, in the open market. They said that the Dniester flowed with Jewish blood.

"Then the second *Aktion* began on April 12, 1942. Hundreds were sent to Belzec and were gassed to death. They took away your father (your mother had already died of Typhus). Then, there was the third and final *Aktion* in September, 1942, when the remaining Jews were marched to the Jewish cemetery, shot and buried there. There were less than fifty who survived in the forced labor camps. There are no Jews in Hustechko! But recently, some *landsleit* gathered money and put up a monument in the cemetery and they are writing a memorial book."

Gittel was astonished, "How did you survive?"

"I did not survive! Look at me! I saw my first husband, Duvid, beaten and taken away to work, but he never returned. My two sons were killed in the second *Aktion.* I hid in a garbage heap on the outskirts of Hustechko and was later hidden at night by a Ukrainian friend of your father. I lived in the garbage heap until the Russians returned. I married Ruven, whom I met in a D.P.Camp, in 1945. Here I am, a dead person trying to live again. We have two beautiful children, a boy and a girl and we live in the West Bronx. I praise God that my little boy is named after my first husband."

GITTEL AND BLIMA became closer friends, for they were the last remnants of Hustechko. Their shared grief and survival would be a testament to their lost world. Gittel sensed all along that her parents had not survived. Ten years after the war, they would have contacted her or Rabbi Perlman. But there was a million in one chance that they might have survived behind the Iron Curtain, unable to send messages, and she would wait by the window to greet them when they returned. She needed the hope of their survival for her own survival. Now she could find closure with her family's tragedy.

When Blima left that evening, Gittel realized that it was time to abandon the ghosts of her past that haunted her life. She was Gittel, the wife of Louis Friedman, who lived on Vyse Avenue - not Gittel, granddaughter of Huna Rudnick of Hustechko, privileged Jew under Emperor Franz

Josef. She was blessed with a good husband, a safe place to live, strength to cope with her Diabetes, thank God, and a future for her children.

This was the American dream for which she had left her home in the Old Country. Though her life in America would dominate her thoughts, she would cherish the happy and joyous moments of her youth in Hustechko. That, the Nazis could never destroy. From that day on, Gittel was rarely seen by the window.

Charles H. Freundlich

BREINA

WHEN BREINA was born, she was a source of great joy and disappointment. Her father, Rabbi Shmuel Heller, a graduate of the famous Lubliner Yeshiva in Poland, had wanted a son to whom he could impart his vast Talmudic erudition and continue the family name. Her mother, Ida, was told after the birth, that she could no longer conceive. Ida was thirty years old when she married Rabbi Heller. Her father, a successful corset manufacturer promised his future son-in-law a dowry of three thousand dollars a year for five years, in addition to a brownstone building he owned on Vyse Avenue, to be used for their residence and a *shul*.

49

Charles H. Freundlich

Rabbi Heller had arrived from Poland three years earlier, and he immediately shaved his beard, exchanged his frock coat for a modern suit, and was soon appointed to a pulpit on the Lower East Side of Manhattan. His Yiddish was classic, almost *Litvish,* and bore only a small trace of a Polish accent. His English had improved and was already superior to that of most of his congregants, thanks to his daily reading of the New York Times.

But Rabbi Heller did not fully comprehend or appreciate the new and strange democratic values of America. Here, his congregants, mostly workers - tailors and shoemakers - as he thought of them, were the boss. Even more absurd, money (not piety or Talmudic erudition), defined status! These values were abhorrent to him and to the Polish milieu of his youth. It was humiliating to him - a scion of six generations of rabbis - to be subservient to these unlearned, common people. After a brief and uneventful two years, his contempt for his congregants was manifest, and his position was terminated, with little regret.

Fortunately for him, a congregant, (one of his few admirers), told him about Mr. Rosenberg and his unmarried thirty-year old daughter, Ida. He was hardly twenty-eight, well-built and short, with dark eyes and brown hair. His years in the yeshiva, with long hours on meager rations and little sunshine, had taken its toll, and he appeared much older. It was *bashert* – destined from God - that this *shidduch* [match] was a golden opportunity for him to be independent, with his own shul, and a steady flow of money for five years. His marriage would enable him to return to his authentic self. He regrew his beard and wore a black frock coat as behooves a Talmudic scholar from the Lubliner Yeshiva.

Vyse Avenue

His arrival on Vyse Avenue, and the opening of his *shtiebel* [privately owned shul], was greeted with mixed and powerful emotions. Some locals were alarmed to see a bearded rabbi on their streets. This was America! The Great Depression was still the overriding concern of the people who had placed their hope and faith in Roosevelt, and the *beard* had no place here. This was The Bronx - lined with fashionable apartment buildings and grand three-story brownstones on one side. The Jews had long left the crowded and squalid streets of the Lower East Side. Rabbi Heller's arrival was a throwback to the *shtetl*, the East European small town milieu, that they despised and crossed the ocean to forget.

The brownstone afforded ample space for the new *shtiebel*. The ground floor had been remodeled, and was large enough to accommodate sixty congregants. The Hellers lived on the second floor and they rented out the third floor to an elderly couple. The basement was also remodeled to have their *Kiddushes*, [collations], with wine, cake and herring, and also, for *shalosh seudos* [the Sabbath third meal]. The three front windows were painted with Jewish Stars with a blue background to afford privacy.

On top of the front entrance was a modest sign: "Bet Knesset -Rabbi Shmuel Heller- Services held daily, morning and evening, Sabbaths and Holidays." Metal folding chairs were lined from the back to the middle, where the *tevah* [raised table], held the Torah scroll to be read. The Holy Ark contained one Torah scroll, a gift from Ida's father and mother; the red velvet Ark Cover was blank, waiting for a suitable donor. The ambiance was cozy and informal, congenial to the modest tastes of the worshippers who were uncomfortable with the formality and decorum of the larger institutional synagogues.

After remodeling of the main floor, many people from the neighborhood came to worship and to inspect the new shul. What the shul lacked in class or grandeur, was compensated with the personal warmth and attention that Rabbi Heller afforded every congregant. They felt he was their *Rebbe* and cared about them. Within a month, the Sabbath services included more than fifty men and fifteen women, who were seated behind the cheese cloth *mechitzah*, [partition], de rigueur for an Orthodox shul.

The *kiddushes* were prepared and served by Ida whom everyone called the *Rebbitzen,* following the Sabbath services and included a large pot of hot *chulent*, a bean and potato stew, in addition to the wine and cake. It was unlike the larger Bryant Avenue Synagogue where appeals for money were made every holiday and those unable to donate found themselves marginalized. In addition, Rabbi Heller personified the traditional Orthodox faith of their *shtetls* and the informal and soulful *davening* [worship]. They had no professionally trained cantor and this afforded the wannabe cantors an opportunity to demonstrate their talents.

Rabbi Heller knew each of his congregants by name and place of birth. People felt loved, and this sense of belonging to a close community pervaded the entire service. Rabbi Heller had quickly assimilated the most important principal of leadership: "make your congregants feel good and they will come and be faithful." Attendance increased, and within a year, *Heller's Shtiebel,* as it was called, was endorsed on Vyse Avenue and well-regarded by the entire Jewish community.

"All of this success, I owe to you my dear Rebbitzen," Rabbi Heller asserted. "Who would have dreamed - only a few years ago while I was fleeing the poverty and ant-Semitism of Poland - that God would bless me with such joy and happiness? Praised be God. This is truly a blessed land."

"You did it yourself, with your love for people and your knowledge of Torah," Ida responded.

Ida was obedient and devoted to her husband; though she realized that she was respected, not loved. Her father had bought her a husband and she was grateful that she would not have to bear the ignominy of being an old maid.

She served her husband's meals on time; and when he entered his book-lined study, she did not disturb him. She attended the *mikvah,* the ritual bath, every month, though her husband rarely made love to her. But she was satisfied that she was respected, and had status - a Rebbitzen of a learned rabbi - a scholar of the renowned Lubliner Yeshiva. She poured her love and attention on Breina, sweet Breina, who was her great comfort. But Breina was more attached to her father.

Rabbi Heller's shul was filled every Sabbath morning and even the humblest worshipper donated at least two dollars for an a*liyah,* or even for lifting the Torah. On their *yahrzeits*, a bottle of whiskey and a loaf of sponge or honey cake were offered. In the evenings, Rabbi Heller was working on his study of the laws of *tsitsis* [the fringes for the prayer shawl], and this would be his *magnum opus*, dedicated to the memory of his father, Boruch Yitzhak, of blessed memory. With the success of his *shtiebel,* Rabbi Heller was comforted; the tragedy that he would have no son was mitigated. God had willed that his wife, Ida, though fastidious in observing all the laws of modesty in sex, dress and speech, would bear only one child.

Rabbi Heller was endowed with a sonorous baritone voice, and on New Moons and Holidays, he conducted the services. People loved his *nusach,* the traditional prayer chants, of Poland and of his yeshiva. He did not preach on Sabbath mornings, but offered words of Torah during the afternoon third meal. During the services there was little decorum; people whispered, joked and moved about, greeting each other. Rabbi Heller said, "Let the people talk, as long as they attend services and pray."

Among the worshippers, was Louis Friedman, who lived across the street, and became a *Hassid*, a zealous devotee of Rabbi Heller; and he would attend punctually at 9:00 A.M. every Sabbath. Upon returning home, he would report to his wife, Gittel, all the latest news and gossip of the shul. Gittel was happy that Louis had achieved a sense of importance, but objected to his frequent donations to the shul - as much as two dollars!

Louis' children did not attend the Heller Shtiebel. They began Hebrew School at the Bryant Avenue synagogue and attended its Junior Congregation. These services were led by Jackie and Nate, two students of Yeshiva College, who had a winning way with the youth, told humorous tales and introduced them to the traditional melodies. The experience was most exciting and uplifting for the youth. Sol Friedman, ten years old, was enamored with the Sabbath services and attended every week and began to view the two leaders as his heroes.

Vyse Avenue

The idyllic, serene world of Vyse Avenue was shattered in 1939, when Germany invaded Poland. The families of Gittel Friedman and others, who remained in Poland, were being slaughtered. Attendance at Heller's Shtiebel increased as did other synagogues in the area. In 1941, when Breina was five, the Japanese attacked Pearl Harbor, and America was at war. Breina sensed that she was no longer the center of her father's affection. What would be the destiny of the famous Lubliner Yeshiva and the millions of Jews in Poland? Rabbi Heller's major efforts were no longer directed to his shtiebel. He felt deep anxiety about the safety of his extended family in Poland. Breina did not fathom the cataclysmic change in the world and was frustrated by the diminishing attention of her father.

On Sabbath mornings, guests remained after services for the *chulent* Kiddush. It was a festive experience with singing and laughter - but Ida and Breina were excluded from the ceremony. Ida served the food, and then exited. Breina had tried to intrude into the Kiddush, but she was gently shooed away by her father, who kissed her on her cheek. Once, she returned and her father expressed embarrassment, pinching her on the cheek; Breina left the room sobbing. She yearned for her father's exclusive, unconditional love.

Later in the afternoon, there began a series of visits by young yeshiva students who studied Talmud with the rabbi. Breina observed the attention and warmth with which each young boy was greeted and taken into the rabbi's study. The lessons lasted for an hour and the boys promised to return the following Sabbath. Once again, Breina was excluded; Talmud study was not for girls, she was told.

Breina's reduced status was to change the following year. She received outstanding grades in her first year at the Beth Jacob School and her teacher called Rabbi Heller with great excitement. "Breina is a genius. She has memorized the entire text of the *Sidrah Bereishis.*" Rabbi Heller was astounded. How is it possible for a little girl to be a genius? The Talmud declared that a woman's mind was inferior; it was unnatural for a woman to have a superior intelligence.

That evening, when Rabbi Heller reviewed Breina's lessons, it was apparent she had an extraordinary talent to recall facts, translations, and interpretations of the text. Could it be, he thought, that God has blessed me with more than a brilliant son.

The following week, the visitations of the boys in the afternoon, were cancelled. Rabbi Heller would henceforth devote his time with Breina in the complex study of Talmud. Why not? Was not Beruriah, the wife of Rabbi Meir, a renowned scholar and authority of the law? Breina loved studying Talmud with her father, her teacher. She loved him more than anything else in the world. Her perfect recall of the Talmudic texts, each week, brought her father much pleasure. She enjoyed his touch and the masculine smell of his breath as he spoke to her. While she and the other girls in her class were studying *Humash,* she was studying Talmud every Sabbath with her father.

Ida was pleased that Breina was advanced in her Jewish studies. Ida was conversant in Hebrew and the prayers, but not familiar with the world of the Talmud. But she was unhappy that Breina became estranged from the other girls in her class. She no longer attended the youth club on Sabbath afternoons where they would learn songs and hear *musar*, ethical stories, from the group leaders. On every Sabbath afternoon, she stayed home and studied with her father. Was this normal? Breina was a child and needed to socialize and have amusement. Talmud was a serious endeavor, an arduous burden and discipline for boys preparing to become rabbis.

Ida spoke to her husband, "Breina is a still a child. All she does is study Talmud, Talmud and more Talmud. She has time to grow up. She needs friends. Let her have fun with the other girls."

"My dear, you don't understand. Breina has a special gift - one in a million. She can make us all proud. The name of the Lubliner Yeshiva will be glorified. She is not like other girls; she does not need to play."

Ida realized that her husband was out of touch with American life. Born in America, she imbibed the ideal of the right to personal happiness, and to enjoy one's youth. Life was not just performing *mitzvos* - even the mitzvah of Talmud Torah.

Breina's Talmudic studies with her father continued unabated in their intensity. At sixteen, Breina graduated from High School; her body filled out, and she was ready for college, and meeting young men. But Rabbi Heller opposed her going to college. Instead, she was sent to an Orthodox Teacher's Seminary in England for two years.

Breina's leaving home compelled Rabbi Heller to confront the meaning of his own life and his marriage to Ida. He had no joy, and felt no passion for his wife. She was a good woman, but he needed more to satisfy his manly yearnings. He reflected, I'm still young and virile and only forty-five. Dare I divorce Ida? That would be a *shandeh*, a scandal, that his congregants would not tolerate. And how would Breina feel? Finding a suitable match would be more difficult. Respectable Orthodox families did not intermarry with those disgraced with the stigma of divorce.

The month following Breina's departure for England, Rabbi Heller invited his former students to visit him on Shabbos afternoons. He found their presence a great comfort as if these young boys were his own. He reviewed their Talmud studies and complimented them on their progress. He was very fond of all of them, and devoted his time to each - privately in his study.

When the door of the study was closed, Ida knew that her husband must not be disturbed. When the next student arrived, he waited in the living room. The three young boys, hardly twelve years old, were like his children. Their parents were pleased that Rabbi Heller took such a personal interest in them. And like a father, he often caressed them and placed his arm around their shoulders when they sat next to him. Sometimes, he felt a stirring within, as he held a boy close. What was happening? He felt his pulse increase and his breathing became heavier. When the lessons were over, Rabbi Heller was deeply troubled and conflicted by his own desire to hold the boys close to his own body. He suspected that the *yetzer hara*, the evil impulse, had made him captive of his own erotic needs.

After the two-year program, Breina returned home. Rabbi Heller was delighted to behold an eighteen year old young lady, mature physically, suitable for marriage and bearing children. But Breina was not interested in meeting prospective young yeshiva boys. She loved her father and insisted that he continue his studies in Talmud with her. Ida became alarmed that Talmud study had imprisoned Breina's life.

Was the object of Breina's passion her own father? Ida argued fiercely with her husband to terminate his studies with her. Breina was home for more than three months and had not looked for a job, applied for college or accepted a single offer from one of the marriage brokers. Rabbi Heller pleaded with Ida to have patience. She had to find herself, her own way in life, because she was a gifted scholar - not a normal girl.

Ida was tormented with Breina's refusal to abandon her father's bizarre plans for her Talmud studies. Where could she turn for help? She was embarrassed that her husband, respected by the entire community, was a fanatic - manipulating his own daughter for his own unrealized goals as a Talmudic authority. Perhaps, she mused, I should seek counsel from the Zamushka Rebbe, who held court near the Grand Concourse. Yes, her friend, Dorothy, had found the Rebbe helpful when her marriage was threatened by her husband's obsessive gambling.

Ida's meeting with the Rebbe, the following week, was comforting. Her burden of fear and anxiety was now shared. The secret of her husband's delusions was out. The Rebbe was less concerned with Breina's Talmud study than with the fact that she was not amenable to meeting prospective grooms. This was unacceptable for an Orthodox girl, and was contrary to Torah law. The Rebbe assured Ida that her husband, a *tzaddik,* would do what was proper for Breina. Patience was needed. Ida's anxiety was unwarranted; she needed faith that God would provide a suitable groom for Breina. The Rebbe offered his blessing to Ida and her family:

"God will provide for His holy people. Within the year Breina will, with God's help, find her *bashert,* her destined groom.

After Ida left, the Rebbe called his *shamas*, Zalman, and asked to see the list of parents looking for suitable brides and grooms. Zalman reminded the Rebbe of the Shapiro family, worried that their twenty-five year old son, who had finished college, and was more interested in furthering his career than marriage.

"Not *frum* [pious] enough. The family for the Hellers must have a background in Torah learning. What about the young man from Yeshiva College who finished medical school?"

"Howard Demkin. He's still available. The boy is *frum* and the parents are very comfortable."

Ida was not confident that God would provide. Her dilemma with her husband's fanaticism was unbearable. Something had to be done sooner. She thought about her friend, Gittel, the woman in the window, who lived across the street. Gittel offered a welcoming smile and cheerful word to all who passed her way. Ida waited for Wednesday, when Rabbi Heller would attend his meetings with the other Orthodox Rabbis in the Bronx.

When she passed Gittel's window, she stopped and asked to chat with her privately. Gittel was delighted, "It's a great honor to have the Rebbitzen in my home." Ida tried to withhold her tears. After being seated, she began to vent her feelings.

"But Breina is only eighteen. Is she ready for marriage?" Gittel asked.

"That's not the problem. She's doing nothing to prepare herself for living in a real world. She's becoming a book and lives in the strange and complicated text of the Talmud - and the Talmud, the ancient laws of Babylonia, is not the real world. Even worse, she has become totally engrossed by the rabbi. She has no girlfriends. She's not interested in meeting *anyone* - not interested in going *anywhere.*"

"Have you seen the Zamushka Rebbe?"

"I met with him last week, and he offers comfort and blessings - but no real solutions. I know that others have come to him with marriage problems. Maybe, just maybe, he'll have a groom for Breina."

"I think you need a little patience. Breina is young, and she will change. Your husband is a wise and holy man. Louis always tells me about his beautiful sermons every Shabbos. I'm sure things will work out."

Ida was offered hope and pleasant words but no understanding of the profound personal grief she felt. She would try to have a little more patience. Perhaps the Rebbe was right.

The following week, Rabbi Heller received a call from the Zamushka Rebbe: "My dear and honored *chaver.* One of my congregant's sons has come home for the week-end. The young man is Orthodox, completed Yeshiva College and Medical School and plans to be a psychiatrist. I believe it was Harvard Medical School. I was thinking of your very talented and beautiful daughter."

"Thank you, Rebbe. Let me discuss this with Breina. Thank you. I will call next week."

Rabbi Heller called Ida with a sardonic voice.

"It was the Zamushka Rebbe."

Ida was alarmed, "Is there a problem?"

"No problem, only a request," Rabbi Heller answered. "He has a prospective groom for Breina, a psychiatrist, no less. Breina dear, can you imagine being married to a psychiatrist?"

"It's crazy," Breina responded.

Ida interjected "But he's a graduate of Yeshiva College and Harvard. What's wrong with a psychiatrist?"

Rabbi Heller laughed. "They say all psychiatrists are a little crazy."

"I can wait, Daddy."

Ida felt dismayed at their reaction. She mused: No one is good enough for Breina as long as she's married to the Talmud. The situation is intolerable, if a Harvard graduate is not good enough for her.

"I'll phone the Zamushka Rebbe tomorrow and thank him for his interest in you," Rabbi Heller concluded the conversation.

The following proposals for a lawyer, stockbroker, and accountant also met with disapproval by Rabbi Heller.

"You must not rush into marriage," the Rabbi told his daughter. "You are only eighteen. There is plenty of time."

"I don't need to get married, father. I love you," was her response. She kissed her father and embraced him. Rabbi Heller blushed and was embarrassed by Breina's affection.

The Heller Shtiebel was growing and people often walked more than six blocks to attend services. Notably admired, was the *shalosh seudos,* the festive third meal, when Rabbi Heller would lead in the Hassidic melodies he learned as a youth followed by his popular exposition of the

Torah portion. Breina made her presence known by serving the assortment of herring, cakes and beer.

Once, at a *shalosh seudos*, Breina offered a brief discourse on the Torah portion and the congregants were awestricken. "Breina would make a great rabbi, if only she were a man." But Breina thought to herself, if I were a man I would not have the love of my father.

When Sukkot approached, Breina set up the Sukkah in the backyard of the shul. "See father. Could a son have built a more beautiful Sukkah?" All the children on Vyse Avenue, and even from Home Street, came to visit the Sukkah, where they were given cookies, chocolate bars, and small cups of sweet wine. Breina instructed the children how to hold the *lulav* and *esrog,* the palm leaves and citron, the symbols of the harvest, and make the proper blessings with them. She had become the rabbi's assistant for the neighborhood children, and it became an annual tradition for them to visit the "Breina Sukkah."

One evening, following the High Holidays, Ida complained of dizziness. She had become depressed over the pathological relationship between her daughter and her husband. A doctor prescribed sleeping pills and this provided some relief. But in the morning, Ida failed to cope with the pain of her deep anxiety. She spent more time chatting with Gittel across the street, but avoided talking about Breina. She began to experience fatigue and slept during the day. Rabbi Heller noticed the lack of energy in his wife.

"Dear, you must see Dr. Schatz. You don't look well."

"I'm alright. It's just the stress of the holidays. I'll see Dr. Schatz next week."

Ida would do nothing to mar the joy of the holiday season and place another burden upon her husband. But the intensity of her headaches in the evening became intolerable. She needed more rest. She scrutinized the bottle of sedatives. Then, she seized the bottle and swallowed all the pills.

The following morning, Ida did not stir. Rabbi Heller called Dr. Schatz who lived close by. It was too late. Dr. Schatz told the Rabbi that Ida had died of heart failure. The very suspicion that Ida had taken her own life would have been a scandal - an unpardonable sin that would preclude a public funeral, and cast a deep stain on her family. Dr. Schatz had a traditional religious background and concealing the truth about Ida's suicide, he felt, would be better for the family and the community.

The funeral attracted hundreds of people from the neighborhood and a number of prominent rabbis from the East Side, former friends of Rabbi Heller. The Zamushka Rebbe came, and his passionate eulogy moved many to tears. "The Rebbitzen was truly a *tzedekes*, a righteous woman, an *eishes chayil*, a woman of valor." The burial took place in the New Montefiore Cemetery in Long Island. Five limousines transported the distinguished rabbis and relatives.

Now, there was just the two of them - Rabbi Heller and Breina. More marital offers to Breina were turned down. The rabbi needed Breina to manage the house and serve the constant flow of guests to his shul. Theirs was a special relationship. The rabbi was incapable of independent living. Marry again? What for? He had all the love from Breina and his many devoted congregants.

During the next few years, the composition of the neighborhood changed. Hispanics and Blacks were moving in; and Jews were moving out to the West Bronx and Pelham Parkway. The congregation began to dwindle; and even the prestigious Bryant Avenue Synagogue relocated to Pelham Parkway. The Heller Shtiebel struggled to have a *minyan* on the Sabbath.

Rabbi Heller was in the prime of his life; and his world was dying for the second time. One evening, upon returning from a rabbinic meeting, a young man attacked him and stole his gold watch and wallet. He was bruised slightly when he fell to the concrete, but the trauma of being mugged vitiated his confidence to go out alone at night. Breina admonished him about the dangers of the street, day and night.

One morning, Breina opened the front door after hearing a woman screaming, "Help, help!"

"It's time to leave," declared Breina. "The neighborhood has deteriorated." Rabbi Heller was alarmed. Start all over? No! He would end his life and vocation in his shtiebel on Vyse Avenue.

As the months passed, Rabbi Heller felt the full calamity of his vanishing world. There was neither bliss nor satisfaction. There was no future. Without hope, there was no purpose in struggling to go on.

Six months later, Rabbi Heller had his first heart attack and spent more than a week in the hospital. A month later, he had a fatal heart attack. There were few congregants left in the neighborhood to attend his funeral – neither the Zamushka Rebbe who was ill - nor his Bronx colleagues who had left the area.

At the rabbi's *yahrzeit*, the anniversary of his death, Louis Friedman, one of his most ardent admirers, with his wife Gittel, made the one-hour trip to Long Island to visit the Heller grave. They observed Breina sitting on a bench with a prayer book in her hands. Gittel approached Breina and exclaimed, "What a sense of loyalty and devotion to honor the memory of your wonderful father."

"He was my life," Breina responded.

"But spending all these hours at the cemetery is more than necessary. You are young. It's time to move on. After a full year, you have already proven yourself a faithful and loving daughter."

"*Daughter* - you must be mistaken - I am Rebbitzen Heller!"

THE PENITENT

THREE YEARS after losing Rachel, his only child, Arnold Bergman's wife, Edith, was diagnosed with Breast Cancer. Though Arnold was not a religious man, he felt that God had made an egregious error. His daughter, Rachel, was only five when she was killed in an auto accident. He had warned her numerous times not to cross the street alone, and now, Edith was facing a painful death. Arnold thought that the world was supposed to be good. He had survived, unscathed, the bloodiest Pacific operations of the Second World War, and returned to his family, finished college, and was a successful accountant. The Korean War was over, and Ike was President. If all was well in the world, why had a hell descended upon him? A neighbor, Mrs. Gottlieb, who lived on the same floor of his Art-Deco apartment building in the West Bronx, informed him that when her daughter could not conceive, she went to the Zamushka Rebbe, off the Concourse, for his blessing. Nine months later, a miracle happened. "My daughter, Diane, God should protect her from the evil eye, became pregnant and had a girl."

"Maybe it was a coincidence?" Arnold demurred.

"No. My daughter tried for three years. She even went to a psychologist."

"Maybe her husband was sterile?"

"Are you kidding?" Mike was built like a football player. Besides, the following year they had a boy."

"Did you have to pay the Rebbe?"

"Pay, shmay, I would give a million to have a grandchild."

Arnold was not convinced. He did not believe in miracles and thought the Rebbe was a charlatan preying on people's misery. But what did he have to lose? The doctors had not given him any hope for a cure. He would give the Rebbe a shot.

He came to the two-story brownstone building where the Rebbe held court. He was seated in the waiting room when the *shamus*, an elderly bearded man wearing a black fedora and a tawdry jacket, an open white shirt that needed laundering, and without a tie, approached him.

"I wish to have the blessing of the Rebbe," Arnold said with reserve.

"What is the nature of your problem?" the *shamus* asked.

68

"My wife has Breast Cancer - how much for the blessing?

"That depends."

"Depends on what?"

"Is the cancer in one or two breasts?"

Arnold was nonplussed. "What's the difference?"

"One breast blessing, is $50.00, two breasts, $75.00"

Arnold felt nauseous, "Why not $100?"

"The Rebbe is very compassionate to cancer patients."

"Will you take a check?"

"The Rebbe prefers cash. I'll write out your request and give it to the Rebbe."

Arnold felt like a sucker, but he had crossed his Rubicon. He paid the shamus in five-dollar bills and then entered the Rebbe's office. It was lined with dark wooden book-cases filled with large leather bound volumes, a lectern and a large photo of another bearded rabbi. The Zamushka Rebbe was seated in a high-backed upholstered chair behind a glass covered desk with a telephone. He was an elderly man with a full, scraggly grey beard that left only his eyes exposed, and was dressed in a black caftan.

"Sholom Aleichem, my child, "the Rebbe greeted him. "How can I help you?"

"Sholom Aleichem, Rebbe. My wife is gravely ill. She has cancer. I ask the Rebbe to pray for her. Perhaps she will be blessed with a cure."

"Cancer is a terrible disease. I understand your pain. My first wife, Zlotte, of blessed memory, also passed away from this terrible disease. I prayed for six months and fasted every Monday and Thursday, but it was God's will that she return to the true Eternal World with the righteous of our people. Now, if my father, of blessed memory, the Second Zamushka Rebbe had prayed for Zlotte, God would have immediately sent a cure. Alas, my dear father, of blessed memory, was *niftar*, left us, the year before. I shall be visiting his grave in Montefiore Cemetery next week, and I shall submit your wife's name to be healed in my prayers."

A thought raced through Arnold's mind; if the Rebbe's prayers did not cure his own wife's cancer, how would he cure my Edith?

The Rebbe anticipated Arnold's objection. "We can only pray and hope. We leave it all in God's hand. Sometimes, prayer and *tzedakah* avert the evil decree. Sometimes, the evil decree is too powerful for the Rebbe's prayer. Thus, my Zlotte was not cured. The Talmud declares that there is no death without sin, no pain without sin. One must do penitence and good works every day."

The Rebbe patted Arnold's hand and blessed him. He would pray for Edith, (in Hebrew, Itah bas Henya). He urged Arnold to pray every morning in a *minyan* at shul, do penitence, recite the complete Book of Psalms, and above all, to observe all the *mitzvos*.

"God desires the heart. Prayer is the service of the heart. Your generous gift will help the poor and needy and especially those who devote their lives to the study of Torah."

Arnold had not attended synagogue for years, except on Yom Kippur, in deference to the memory of his parents who had brought him up in the Orthodox tradition. He decided to attend morning *minyan* which began at 6:30 A.M. at the local shul, which ended with enough time for him to take the subway and arrive on time at his office on Thirty-Seventh Street. He felt misplaced among the elderly men at the minyan who rattled off the prayers like tobacco auctioneers, while he read the English translation silently. He noted three other younger men who said *Kaddish* and slowly lost his sense of being an outsider. Arnold was a young man, thirty-five, and he was strong and would surmount his tragedies. He had a life to live.

Three months later, Edith died. He regretted the sum of money he had given to the Zamushka Rebbe, the hours wasted at shul, and the chanting of the Psalms. He thought: Edith was a saint. She lit candles every Friday eve and kept a Kosher home. She never failed to place a few coins in the *pushke* for the *schnorers* who knocked on her door. She even observed the laws of *family purity*, of separation from sex during her monthly period, in accordance with Orthodox tradition, and her mother's instructions.

When she was told of her cancer, she said to Arnold, "I'm not dying. I died when Rachel was killed. My life was over then. Take care of yourself, and say Kaddish for me."

Like most victims of grief, Arnold began to rationalize and bargain with God. Perhaps God did not hear my prayers because of my years of being an *apikores* [non-believer]. I had abandoned God and the faith of my parents. Edith was innocent and pure. Was God punishing me? Perhaps if I were more attentive to my father's ways, the Shabbos and all the rest of the outdated customs of the Old Country, God would bless me; God would give me a second chance. Maybe my own life would be granted some happiness.

Charles H. Freundlich

Arnold's humdrum life as an accountant on Thirty-Seventh Street had provided him and his family with a decent living. But it was dull, routine, devoid of passion. When he returned home to Edith and his little daughter, Rachel, there was a sublime joy. Now, they were both gone. His parents were dead and he had little expectation that things would improve. There was no sense of purpose in his life. He had no motivation to get out of bed in the morning. What for? To return to his dreary office in the garment district?

In his desperation, Arnold thought of a plan. He would do penitence; start all over by going back to his youth. He would return to his old neighborhood in the East Bronx, where he spent his youth with his religious parents on Vyse Avenue, and become a *ba'al teshuva,* a penitent, to Orthodoxy.

He recalled his youth and some of the very joyous moments on Friday evenings and holidays in the modest four-room apartment. His father, Zelig, was an unsophisticated, pious Jew who relished a warm bath and the traditional Sabbath meal with stuffed chicken every Friday evening. He especially enjoyed the very noisy and informal services at shul, where he served as *shamus,* caretaker, Torah reader and keeper of the books.

Zelig made a modest salary working in the shul. But with the extra donations: selling *esrogim* on Sukkos, wine on Pesach, and candles for Hanukkah - it was adequate to survive and he was satisfied. Though not a *talmid chacham*, a Talmudic scholar, Zelig was a man of pure faith and little doubt - who never ate without making the proper blessing before every meal, and donned *tallis* and *tefillin* every morning at the minyan.

Vyse Avenue

Arnold would attend services in his father's old shul, known as *Anshei Horodenka*, a store-front with painted glass on Bryant Avenue near Freeman Street. He, the son of Zelig Bergman, would reclaim his heritage. Surely, there would be some of the older congregants who remembered his father, if not him, (though, he had celebrated his Bar Mitzvah there many years earlier).

It was not difficult finding an apartment on Vyse Avenue. Many residents were abandoning the neighborhood and he needed only one bedroom. His new apartment was on the first floor, a few blocks from the shul. When he returned one afternoon from work, he noticed a woman at the window on the ground floor, her chest and arms resting on a pillow on the window-sill. It was Gittel Friedman, who was a fixed presence on the block for many years. As Arnold passed her he said, "Don't stare. It's me Arnold. Remember me? I'm Zelig's son."

"Sure, I remember Zelig, the *Tzaddik.* What happened all these years? You never came around to visit. Are you too good for us? You used to play Stickball. Zelig was a gentleman and your mother, Yetta, was an *eishes chayil*, a wonderful *balabusta.* They were the most Orthodox people in the white building next door. Your parents were from Galicia, not far from my town."

Arnold was delighted to know that his parents were still remembered by the neighbors.

"I don't play Stickball anymore."

"Of course, you grew up. I thought you got married. How is your wife?"

"Edith died recently."

"I'm so sorry. God should protect us."

"And before her, my baby, Rachel died. She was only five. I felt so depressed, without Edith in the house in the West Bronx. I had to get away. You know the saying, 'change your place and you change your luck.' I live on the first floor. How have you been? How's your family?"

"Thank God, nothing to complain. I just received letters from Seymour and Marvin from Korea. They'll both be home next month. Thank God they didn't see any action. And Sol - you'll never believe - was just ordained in Jerusalem by the Chief Rabbi of Israel. He'll be home from Israel at the end of June. God be praised, there was no war with Egypt. If only my husband Louis was well. You know, he had an operation on his colon for cancer last year. They say it was a success."

"Cancer, I know well. It robbed me of my Edith. I also remember your daughter, Elaine, a teenager."

"A teenager - she's married and has two beautiful boys. They live in Jersey. She calls me every day."

"Wonderful. Have to be getting along. Speak to you later, Gittel."

"Where's the fire? Maybe you'll have dinner with us this Shabbos?'

"Thanks. I'll let you know. I have to get settled first."

Arnold needed to be alone. He needed privacy, and didn't want to deal with all the personal questions from Gittel and the other neighbors who remembered his parents. He needed time to reclaim his past - the past he thought he left behind.

When he entered the shul Shabbos morning, he recognized Mr. Geller, who had aged - was slightly stooped, and with grey hair. He recollected the faces of other old-timers, but had forgotten their names. They were looking at him, a new-comer to the shul. He introduced himself as Zelig's son, yes, Zelig the Shamus. They cheered and smiled. They remembered his father, deeply devoted to the shul and a hard worker. Some said that Zelig was one of the *lamed vuvniks* [thirty-six righteous men], who sustain the world.

It was a novelty to see a younger man in the shul among the elderly, (those unable to move west when the neighborhood began to deteriorate). Most of the metal folding chairs were not occupied. The old Rabbi Gruss, a Litvak, was gone, and the congregation was now led by Rabbi Lustig, a Polish survivor of the Holocaust, who was also a tailor in mid-town. He served the shul part-time, and he satisfied the dwindling congregation.

Arnold quickly integrated into the group, and hoped to ingratiate himself by attending morning minyan which began at 7:00 A.M., and also on every Sabbath and holiday. As a regular, he was noticed - especially since he was well-tailored and much younger than the others. His English was admired by the immigrants from Poland and Russia who spoke Yiddish and accented English among themselves.

The neighborhood, where Jewish immigrants from the Lower East Side had settled thirty years earlier, had declined and lost its prestige. Now, it was populated with Puerto Ricans and Blacks. The increased crime and violence had driven away many of the Jews, Irish and Italians to the West Bronx and the suburbs. The streets were littered with garbage and the sounds of Latino music pierced the air. But it was the home of Arnold's youth, where he grew up and went to school, and he felt a sense of rootedness and belonging.

Charles H. Freundlich

After attending services for six months, he was voted to be the president. Who else could make a *Yizkor* appeal in such impeccable English? The presence of an American–born president would attract the unaffiliated American-born Jews to join the shul, which was desperate for new members. Arnold began to enjoy his rebirth as a religious and observant Jew. He was now a *macher* [big shot], well-respected by the congregation. He could tolerate the je-june work as an accountant in the garment industry. The congregants of *Anshei Horedenka* marveled that Arnold had brought back the spirit of Zelig Bergman, the shamus, with his enthusiasm and commitment. The shul was being rejuvenated!

As President of the shul, it was his main task to oversee the finances and make the holiday appeals. In addition, he was called upon to support Rabbi Lustig when modern pressures were increasing to breach the wall of Orthodoxy. Most of the congregants had come from religious backgrounds; though, they were not strictly Orthodox. But they wanted their shul and rabbi to be Orthodox. They recalled the religious traditions of the *shtetl* where every Jew knew his duties to God, family, and community, which they observed without question or rational understanding.

New ideas or rituals were not welcome. But was it possible to restrain the currents of modernity which were breaching the ancient walls of tradition?

When a few congregants (smart-asses, according to Arnold) proposed replacing the opaque cloth *mechitzah* [partition], with cheese-cloth, so that the women could see the men, there was a hullabaloo. The *mechitzah,* which separated the men's section from the women's section, was always six feet high with opaque cotton as required by Orthodox law - never mind, that another local Orthodox synagogue on Longfellow Avenue had just lowered the partition to four feet.

The various voices became a cacophony of friction.

"So go to Longfellow Avenue," shouted Mr. Geller.

"This is our shul and we want to modernize," responded Mr. Braun.

"Modernize? Go to the Reform Temple"

"This is America, and a democracy - not Poland. Here, the majority rules."

"We have always had a kosher mechitzah."

"If we don't make any modern changes, we won't have a shul in three years."

"We pay dues. It's our shul and what we say goes!"

They heard that the Conservative synagogues in Long Island had *family seating* - no mechitzah - and were attracting the younger and more educated element. Rabbi Lustig avoided controversy. Not wishing to offend the hot-headed reformers, he called upon Arnold to defend the faith. Arnold could put the rebels in their place by reminding them: "In this shul, Rabbi Lustig is the only and exclusive religious authority! If you don't like it, go elsewhere! This is the shul of my father, Zelig, of blessed memory, and he would not approve of any reforms." The six-foot opaque, cotton *mechitzhah* remained.

A second crisis arose when one of the younger members suggested a change in the menu of the *shalosh seudos*, the third meal, held on Shabbos afternoon. "We are tired of the same herring and onions every week," they argued, "We would like salmon, instead."

Arnold countered, "We have always eaten herring and onions since I was a child. My father, Zelig, of blessed memory, ate herring. That's the way it has always been, and that's the way it's going to be!"

"Your father was a simple *Galicianer.*"

Arnold took hold of Mr. Braun's lapels and began shaking him. Rabbi Lustig intervened.

"True, there is no sin in eating salmon," Rabbi Lustig reasoned. "But once you start making changes, who knows what will be next – maybe no mechitzah, maybe no Hebrew." It was decided that the salmon substitute was too controversial and was postponed indefinitely. Orthodoxy had its champion in Anshei Horedenka; and Arnold Bergman was his name.

Arnold visited the Montefiore Cemetery in Queens at least once a month and chanted the *Moley* prayers by the gravesite of Edith and Rachel. He also chanted the prayers for his parents, and promised to donate charity to honor their memory. On their *Yahrzeits,* he never failed to bring a bottle of whiskey and honey cake for the daily minyan.

Arnold felt that his penitence, his lifestyle transformation, was complete. He had become more passionate about his life. But was he happy? He was unsure of the blessings from God; but certain that his negative feelings of the futility of his life, his chronic depression, were dissipated. He could rise early in the morning with great enthusiasm, thank God for the blessing of life, *modeh ani,* wash his hands with a cup of water, three times to rid the evil spirit, and walk the three blocks to shul, where he was a key member of the minyan. He enjoyed putting on *tefillin,* and, like his father, he wound the leather straps outward on his arm in the Hassidic tradition of the *Galicianas*.

A year had passed since the death of his wife. Kaddish was over, and it was time to begin a new chapter. He was only thirty-six, not bad looking, though he was slightly bald, and a little heavy. But he had a steady job, almost three thousand dollars in the bank, and felt the need to satisfy his libido. He needed a wife.

He had not dated for more than seven years and was apprehensive when he attended the Starlight Ball Room on Saturday night. But he could dance and he approached an attractive woman. She was congenial, almost eager to meet him. Her name was Nancy and she was a teacher at P.S. 20. He spoke about his work and family tragedies. Then she asked him, "Are you Jewish?"

Arnold felt awkward. Was there something wrong with his nose or had he spoken with an accent? He didn't want to lose her. She was pretty and much younger than him. She reminded him of his Edith, with delicate features and was cheerful."

"My name is Arnold Bergman and I'm Jewish."

"Most of my friends are Jewish," Nancy replied. "In fact, most of the teachers at P.S. 20 are Jewish. But religion is not important to me."

Arnold saw beauty in her delicate features and was moved by her soft tone of voice and demure manner. Could he be in love? Not since his wife had died, had he felt so attracted to another woman.

"Could we see each other again? I mean, outside the Ball Room?"

Nancy smiled. "Here's my phone number. I live on Kelly Street."

Arnold did not sleep well that evening, The following Sunday morning, he decided to drive to the Montefiore Cemetery to clarify his feelings. He stood before his father's grave stone and placed a pebble on top.

"Papa, I've become a good Jew and a loyal member of the shul, your shul and now, my shul. I know you would be proud of me. I am happy with my new life, which is like your life. But Edith and Rachel are gone. I am lonely. Last night I met a woman, a teacher. I feel strongly about her and I think I am in love. But she is not religious. Do you understand Papa?"

On Monday, Arnold called Nancy and asked her out for the following Saturday evening. Nancy spoke with reserve, "Arnold, I like you as a friend. You are kind and nice. But, I am twenty-eight and I want to get married. I spoke to my father. He would not accept you. He came from Russia when he was young and discarded his Orthodox faith for socialism. My mother is very secular, like me. I cannot hurt their feelings. It would not work."

"Maybe, if they met me, your parents would like me. I make a good living as an accountant and I have savings. I'm not a fanatic, not so religious."

"You don't know Daddy. He hates religion and religious people. It wouldn't work."

"Maybe, if I were less religious? I can compromise."

"It wouldn't work."

"But you are grown up, an adult, a teacher. Do you have to please your parents?

"It's not that simple. I love Daddy and Mom very much. It wouldn't work. Goodbye."

When Arnold hung up the receiver, he felt he must return to the cemetery and speak to his father. "Papa, I know you will be very proud of me. Last week, I met a very beautiful woman. But she was like a *shiksa,* [Gentile] not very Jewish. Her family was totally assimilated. I think her father was a communist. For a moment I was attracted to her. I even fell in love. But I resisted the temptation to get seriously involved. You know how I prevented the cheese-cloth *mechitzah,* and the salmon for the *shalosh seudos* from corrupting our shul. I have come home again. I feel young again. I feel so close to you and Mamma now. Both of you are close to my heart. But Papa, I am alone. I miss Edith. I have a whole life to live. Please tell God to bless me with a wife. I am thirty-six, so please hurry."

The following Friday when Arnold was walking to shul, he was stopped by Gittel who called from the window. "Arnold, please don't hurry. I want to speak to you."

"I'm on my way to shul for services. Now is not a good time."

"Please, only a minute. I want you to come to my apartment tomorrow for Kiddush."

"Thank you Gittel," But I prefer to make Kiddush in shul."

"Please, Arnold, come to my Kiddush after services. You won't be sorry."

It was hard to say "no," to Gittel, who was adamant.

"Perhaps - another time."

"When Gittel says, 'you won't be sorry', you won't be sorry."

"You win. I'll come tomorrow right after services."

That evening Arnold reflected about the invitation. He felt uncomfortable; perhaps jealous of the Friedman family that thrived as a happy family, despite their poverty.

When Arnold entered the Friedman apartment, after services, the table was set, Louis was seated, and Gittel took his hand and seated him next to an attractive woman. "This is Irene, my Cousin Esther's daughter. You know, my cousins, from Hoe Avenue."

Irene shook hands with Arnold while Louis chanted the Kiddush over wine.

"I live with my daughter, Rachel, near my parents on Hoe Avenue," Irene explained. Arnold was stunned when he heard the name, *Rachel.*

Gittel intervened. "Irene's husband was a soldier and was killed during the war. Rachel was born two months later."

Gittel brought in a large platter of salads: salmon, egg and coleslaw.

"We eat salmon every Shabbos and tuna during the week," Gittel said.

'"You don't eat herring?" Arnold asked.

"*Herring,* that's for Litvaks," Gittel retorted. "Since we had our grocery store, we learned to eat American - tuna fish salad during the week and expensive salmon salad on Shabbos."

Arnold changed the subject. "I'm an accountant and work in Manhattan. My wife Edith died last year."

"I work in a Manhattan office as a secretary," Irene responded.

"It must have been hard for you after your husband died."

"It was a shock to all of us. Rachel never knew her father. Gittel hasn't missed an opportunity to introduce me, you know. I hope you don't mind"

"*Mind,* I'm grateful to Gittel for thinking of me. Perhaps we can see each other again."

"I would like that."

When the meal was over and Arnold left, Gittel turned to Irene, "What do you think? His father, Zelig, was a *Galiciana* like our people. He was the shamus at Anshei Horedenka, *balebateshe* [refined] people."

"I don't know yet. He's nice. I hope he calls me."

Arnold called Irene the following Monday, and they went to the Loew's Boulevard Theater the following Saturday evening and had ice cream afterwards. She was wearing a fashionable red outfit. Arnold wore a blue serge suit and a grey checked tie. When he took her home, she said, "I had a wonderful evening, Arnold." Arnold kissed her on her cheek.

"I like you, Irene. Can we go out again?"

Four months later, Arnold and Irene were married in the study of the Hoe Avenue shul where her father was well-respected. Irene's parents and her brother attended with Gittel and Louis and their children. Elaine and her husband, Max, came in from Jersey with their boys. It was a small, catered affair held in the vestry of the shul, and Arnold insisted on paying for the meal and the fee for the rabbi.

Gittel exclaimed, "He's generous. A gentleman! A marriage made in heaven!"

"Thanks to you," Louis added.

They made their home on Vyse Avenue, with two bedrooms on the third floor.

Arnold returned to his shul the following Shabbos and proclaimed, "Salmon may be served instead of herring."

THE GREMLINS

SOL STOOD on the sidewalk on Vyse Avenue watching the older teens play Stickball. How powerful and skilled they were, he marveled, to hit the small Spalding with a broomstick, hundreds of feet in the air. They were mighty titans, he reflected. Someday, I will become one of them. He lamented the fact that he stood alone, hardly noticed, as if he were invisible, a nonentity. Someday, they will see me and ask me to join them and play on their teams.

His moment came - and it was one of the most fortunate episodes in his life. Heshy, one of the iconic stars of Vyse Avenue, hit a long fly ball that veered right and landed on the roof of one of the brownstones. Heshy was short, powerfully built, with curly short-cropped hair and a ruddy face, and was one of the most popular guys on the block. He was a power-hitter; and was well-respected among the other teens. This hit was no light matter, for *Spaldings* cost five cents, and most of the players were fearful of ascending the roof to retrieve the balls. Tenants on the third floor constantly warned the players not to ascend their rooftop lest they call the police. The rule of the street was: he who hit the ball must retrieve it, or provide a new ball.

When Sol saw the ball fly over the roof, he ran to Heshy and boasted, "I can get it for you." Heshy smiled, patted Sol on the head and said, "Thanks, you're my friend and pal."

Sol ascended the two flights of stairs, opened the closet door that contained the ladder, climbed it, pushed open the lid, and reached the rooftop, where he spied the Spalding that Heshy hit - and also other balls that lay on nearby rooftops. It was a treasure! He hurled the balls down to the street to Heshy amidst the wild acclaim of the other players.

"You're my pal," Heshy greeted Sol when he returned to the street. Sol felt elated to be noticed by him and the other teens who he admired as leaders of the street community. He esteemed him and the other Stickball stars: Bones, Izzie, Duke, Joel, Schnitz, and Ira, and hoped that he would become one of them when he grew older. These super-stars were his idols and he regarded them with the same exuberance he held for Joe DiMaggio, Mel Ott and Hank Greenberg. His passion to be a star athlete would be a transition from his stodgy existence in his crowded apartment, to public acclaim by his peers.

Vyse Avenue

Sol was not in their league, but he was endowed with natural athletic talent. He could run swiftly, had excellent eye-hand coordination, and most important, a competitive spirit to win. Heshy took him under his wing and he regarded him as his personal friend - though six years of age separated them. With Heshy as his "pal," he would receive protection from some of the older and stronger kids on the block. Thanks to his tutelage, he was included in the games of the older teens as a ball chaser and keeper of the Stickball bats.

Sol was also included in the more physical sports like touch football and roller skate hockey. Heshy was a superb mentor to Sol and taught him some of the basic strategies for street survival: how to protect himself, when there were gang wars, or violence following the games. Stickball provided Sol with a basic scheme for competing in the game of life. His powerful affection for Heshy continued until Pearl Harbor when the draft swept most of the eighteen year olds overseas, and depleted Vyse Avenue of its athletic talent.

Sol's passion for sports and his zeal to be accepted and respected as a star, continued unabated throughout his youth. But most important, he learned that serving as a ball retriever for Heshy, opened the doors for a reciprocal friendship that enhanced his stature on the block. He was astute to comprehend the fundamental law of getting ahead and commanding respect; namely, serving and being useful to others led to valuable relationships. This would be his lodestar for success throughout his life. Talent and knowledge, alone, were no recipes for success unless they were coupled with personal service.

School posed little challenge to Sol who was gifted with a high I.Q., and excelled above the other pupils at P.S. 66. He rarely studied and received little encouragement from his parents to read or strive for improvement. He was attentive during class and was endowed with a photographic memory. He loved his teachers, all female, and especially the order and discipline of the school day. He often recalled the names of his teachers, Mesdames: Dowling, White, Sweeney, Grossberg, and Cohen. He even liked the principal, the venerable Mr. Sussman. Mrs. Grossberg introduced him to the wonders of America, democracy, and citizenship. A child of Jewish immigrants, who spoke Yiddish as their mother tongue, Sol was still uncertain about being an authentic American.

Mrs. Cohen was in charge of the library and was very fastidious. She would call Sol to the side of the room and ask him, discreetly, if he had another white shirt. The collar of the one he was wearing needed laundering. She printed beautifully with her gold-capped, black Parker 51" in the beginning of the term and then changed to a gold-capped brown Schaeffer pen, the following term. Sol noted his teacher's choice of fountain pens as symbols of status and privilege and hoped that sometime in the future, he would own one of them.

School provided the disciplined structure that he did not have at home. He rarely spoke with his parents who were preoccupied with the essentials of survival. He felt closer to his teachers and more comfortable in his classroom than in his crowded apartment. He appreciated his own desk and being a monitor at the school office. He was amiable with the office secretary and was taught to ring the bell and perform other office tasks. He felt a sense of prominence over the other pupils since he was always at the head of his class from first grade though graduation in sixth grade. But his parents took his straight "A" marks for granted. They were more concerned with the lesser grades of his two brothers, Seymour and Marvin.

In sixth grade, love entered Sol's life, and her name was Elaine, (the same as his sister's), who sat in the next row. Most of the other boys were delighted to brag that they had a girlfriend. Sol's infatuation ended at graduation when he was required to attend Junior High School 40, while Elaine was assigned to attend P.S. 98, Herman Ridder Junior High School. Elaine's small photo remained in Sol's graduation autograph album for many years though he never bothered to contact her.

Softball competition in the schoolyard, between the classes, elicited Sol's talent as a hitter and fielder. It was to serve him well when he starred for his Stickball team, the Gremlins.

The apartment buildings on Vyse Avenue were teeming with young married couples who spawned hundreds of youth. They were forced to play on the streets where there was more open space. Of all games, none offered more excitement and prestige than Stickball, an ersatz baseball. Sol could hit a Spalding more than two sewer's distance, and was an excellent fielder on third base. He was often the first to be selected when teams were organized. With at least five players on each team, he was never left out and he basked in the adulation of being in the inner circle of his crowd. Few of the youth owned a baseball glove which was beyond the budget of most families; but a rule of the street required one to share a glove, especially with the third baseman. Sol had the distinction of playing this key position since the narrow streets obviated the need for a short-stop position. Sol had a monopoly to play third base for the Gremlins and was the leading hitter and fielder.

With a surfeit of boys competing to play, permanent teams were formed to ensure inclusion of the best players. When he was eleven, Sol and his friends formed a Stickball team. He suggested the name "Gremlins," and it was accepted by all. The team was a diverse group of Italian, Irish and Jewish kids from public schools who got along together and would compete with the "Robins" - a team of students from St. John's Catholic School on Hoe Avenue. Throughout the summer, the Gremlins and the Robins played each other, often betting as much as five dollars. Despite the fierce competition, the Robins and the Gremlins often met after the games to have egg-creams and pretzels at *Elshin's* candy store.

The best team was led by two brothers - Tom and Georgie, both superb athletes, who lived around the corner on West Farms Road, but played on Vyse Avenue. Similar to the older teenagers down the block, the Gremlins traveled throughout the neighborhood challenging everyone. The length of Vyse Avenue enabled two Stickball games to be played simultaneously – one, "down the block" near Home Street (where the older teenagers played for money on Sunday mornings), and another, to be played "up the block," closer to 167th Street. The teams were not permanent, though the Robins lasted longer, and they were able to purchase their own blue, satin team jackets.

Vyse Avenue

Stickball was the cohesive element in creating a sense of community among the different ethnic and religious youth despite the fact that their parents rarely socialized. There were no Negroes (as they were then called) or Hispanics on Vyse Avenue, and no occasion for racial violence. The adults kept their own prejudices private and all exhibited a sense of neighborliness.

The three metropolitan baseball teams: The Yankees, Giants, and Dodgers, attracted zealous fans who often engaged in heated arguments about the best players. What could be more provocative than being a Brooklyn Dodger fan in the Bronx - the home of the Yankee Stadium? And even more unusual, was a small group of Giant fans who lived in Sol's building and conducted themselves with a sense of special hauteur. The statistics of each major league baseball player were memorized and scrutinized each day. These facts served to provide fuel for the heated confrontations between the various fans.

Very few of the kids were attracted to hockey. Baseball was the main sport and dominated their interests. But Stanley, a bright kid with glasses, played hockey on his roller skates. He knew that only Sol - who was years younger, without skates - would be delighted to play with him. Stanley guided Sol who became a skilled hockey player. He was taught the art of body-checking and lifting the puck. Often, Stanley would approach Sol's building early Sunday mornings, knock on his window with his hockey stick, and beckoned him to come out and play. Once again, Sol's deference to Stanley to play hockey, when no other kids played the game, created a rewarding friendship.

Charles H. Freundlich

There was no protective equipment or padding for the few hockey players, and the hard, rubber puck became a lethal weapon for a skillful player. Stanley, the only player with roller skates, and conscious of his handicap, was rarely body-checked by those running in sneakers. In the heat of the contest, fairness gave way to the pursuit of victory. "Look at Stanley falling on his ass," Marvin shouted with triumph. But Stanley would retaliate by slapping the puck high enough to hit Marvin in the shins and score a delightful sense of justice.

On Sundays, there were major Stickball games. Visiting teams from Bryant Avenue and Southern Boulevard would compete with the cream of Vyse Avenue. These were serious, betting games, where as much as one hundred dollars were awarded to the winners. Bones, a skinny but talented player, knew how to hit the Spalding against the opposite buildings past the cross-section on Home Street. Though not a power-hitter, he was certain to get on base. The team chose him as captain and negotiator for the schedule and betting. Izzy was the star, and he was compared to Mickey Mantle. He, too, was blond, tall and muscular and could hit a ball more than *three sewers*. Batting fourth, Izzy was clean-up man, often driving home the first run. Duke was second only to Izzy in power, hitting a double or a home run. But Heshy was Sol's favorite.

The local home team stars carried themselves with great bravado, and were a source of great excitement on Vyse Avenue. They attracted scores of adult spectators, and their victories were a source of pride for the entire block. They were the champions in the neighborhood - until someone suggested that they play a team of Black guys from Prospect Avenue - about a mile's distance away. The Black players were particularly muscular and athletic, and humiliated the Vyse Avenue team by a score of sixteen to two. The winners went home with more than two hundred dollars! The Vyse Avenue stars were amazed at the superb athleticism of the Blacks. "Since when did colored guys play baseball? Did the major leagues have a single Negro player?" the Vyse team players wondered.

Playing Stickball had its risks. For some inexplicable reason, the police used to confiscate the broomsticks which were used for bats; and warned the kids not to play on the streets. One of the guys was assigned to play "chickie" and alarm the others when a police car was approaching. Sol was dauntless and often ran with the broomstick to his apartment building .

Sol's idyllic life with Stickball was soon to end when religion demanded a larger portion of his personal time and a new life-style. When he enrolled at Hebrew School at the Bryant Avenue synagogue (K'hal Adath Yeshurun, K.A.Y.), he was required to attend four afternoons a week and Sunday mornings.

Sol loved learning about the ancient Bible heroes and the customs and ceremonies of his faith. But he still felt passionate about Stickball and the Gremlins. He admired his Hebrew School teacher, Rabbi Fleischman, who had a wonderful sense of humor and was always cracking jokes about the letters of the alphabet. Rabbi Fleischman seemed to relish his teaching and radiated warmth and closeness to the students with his perennial smile. Sol's time for Stickball was diminished by the daily attendance at Hebrew School and the conflict worsened.

Charles H. Freundlich

One afternoon, after Sol missed an important game against the Robins, a meeting was held in the street. Kelly, who was the captain of the Gremlins, spoke critically to Sol: "The Gremlins have been losing too many games lately. We voted, and decided that we've got to get rid of some of the *crap* on the team. We decided to get rid of you." Sol found the offensive words outlandish and hurtful - and difficult to believe. Only last week, he was considered the stellar third baseman of the Gremlins!

He left the street and took refuge in his bedroom. He pulled down the window shades and sat in silence. He was desolate – rejected, "crap." For more than an hour, he sat on his bed, alone in the darkness. He felt that his life had come to a tragic end. Was there life beyond Stickball?

SOL'S JOURNEY

HEBREW SCHOOL opened up a new world of challenges for Sol and required his weekly attendance at Sabbath Junior Congregation services. He learned many festive prayer-melodies in addition to hearing inspiring sermonettes. He did not have to compete to belong to the Junior Congregation; nor did he have to prove himself a star. The ambiance was one of cooperation, participation and camaraderie. Sol found in Rabbi Fleischman the closeness of a friend, who spoke proper English, loved baseball, and was thoroughly modern.

At the end of the year, Rabbi Fleischman announced that he was leaving his position as principal to become a rabbi in New Hampshire. Sol was distressed, and felt a deep sense of loss; but Rabbi Fleischman assured the students that he would be in contact with them and also visit. He never did. But the impact of the rabbi's vibrant personality and warmth left an indelible mark on Sol's personality and his desire to imbibe more of Jewish studies and rituals.

Rabbi Peskin replaced Rabbi Fleischman as the principal and teacher of the Hebrew School. He was kind and passionate about his work and had a mellifluous voice. But he was very lax with discipline, and the students thought he was feckless. Rabbi Peskin was born in Poland, spoke with a subtle accent, and had graduated from the Jewish Theological Seminary. He left after the year, and was replaced by Rabbi Fox, from Brooklyn, who was young and vivacious. Rabbi Fox transformed the course of Sol's life.

Rabbi Fox was tall, muscular and affable. He was attending Columbia College, and studying towards a medical career. He often spoke about the Jewish community in Brooklyn, where he lived, and the impressive piety of its Orthodox Jews. The Bronx had numerous Orthodox synagogues, but, few observant Orthodox Jews, except for a few old, bearded men. Most of the regulars at *shul* were immigrants from Eastern Europe and spoke Yiddish among themselves, but were not strictly observant.

Rabbi Fox emphasized the importance of *mitzvos,* commandments, that defined the Jewish way of life. Sol was undergoing a profound religious metamorphosis. He began to wear *tsitsis,* the under-shirt garment with four fringes, symbolic of the 613 commandments of the Torah. Next, Sol was making a blessing before the meals, like his father, and wearing a *yarmulka*, a skull cap.

Vyse Avenue

Wearing a cap at all times was the greatest challenge for Sol. Formerly, Sol wore a black skull cap when he ate in his home, and during prayers in synagogue. Now, he was advised that he had to wear a cap in the street. Sol believed that the street was public and secular. A black skull cap, (called a Jew-cap, by some) was not appropriate for the street. On Sabbaths, when he wore a suit, he wore a fedora to synagogue. The winter months presented no problem when most youth wore a knitted cap.

But what was appropriate for spring and summer? Sol learned that many Orthodox boys wore either a baseball cap, sailor hat, or the crown cut out from a fedora. Sol sensed that these caps did not signify a religious symbol and they were kind of queer. He wondered, wasn't this a form of deception? Did he have to conceal his religious identity in public? He wasn't ashamed to be religious. He struggled with this dilemma in public school and when he entered a movie theater or museum. Constantly wearing a cap alienated him from the other boys on the block. But Rabbi Fox explained; it would be a constant reminder that God was with him always, and this made the social inconvenience tolerable.

Rabbi Fox inspired the students with his extraordinary feats of strength. He would bring a spike to school, hold it up to the class, and declare, "With the help of God, I will bend this spike." He asked the class to help him by chanting the *shema* (the fundamental prayer of Judaism) which would give him the Divine power to bend the spike. After a few seconds, the rabbi, turned red, began to bend the spike, and declared victory for the power of prayer.

The students were convinced that Rabbi Fox was endowed by God with extraordinary power. As the weeks passed, Rabbi Fox spoke about the commitment of the ancient rabbis, their martyrdom, over the centuries, to observe the faith in its purity, and how every Jewish youth must be a committed martyr. To neglect the commandments was a betrayal of these rabbis, and two hundred generations of pious ancestors. To cast aside the Jewish faith and traditions, was tantamount to being a traitor and disloyal to God's way. Sol was thoroughly enthralled with the rabbi's passion for Judaism and he wished he could be like him. He must obey the rabbi and continue to add commandments to his daily life and follow in the footsteps of Rabbi Fox who was the voice of God.

Sol's parents were astounded at the sudden transformation of Sol's daily life that seemed retrogressive - a replica of the *shtetl* life they left behind. Gittel said to her husband, "It's a childish phase. He'll grow out of it." They failed to fathom the depth of Sol's spiritual awakening. Sol had adopted a new lifestyle with the observance of *Kashrut* and the Sabbath and was like a new-born person.

Gittel and Louis considered themselves traditional Jews (though not strictly observant), but within the normal parameters of immigrant Jews who had left their former life behind and deemed it imperative to Americanize. Sol insisted that the home become Sabbath observant - no radio or putting on lights on the Sabbath. For his brothers and sister, this seemed an intrusion into their own personal lives and their right to be less observant. Elaine cried, "What will happen to me when my date comes over on Saturday night and finds out that we live in the dark? They'll think that we are crazy fanatics!" But Sol threatened to move out of the house if the Sabbath laws were violated. His parents were reconciled. "Better a crazy house with Sol, than a normal house without Sol," Gittel asserted.

After a while, Gittel and Louis accepted their son's Orthodoxy and were delighted and supportive. Gittel felt that her father and grandfather would be proud to know of their son's turn to tradition and also their enhanced observance. Louis continued to work on the Sabbath and justified it by the necessity of *parnasah*, providing bread for the family. Sol's religious awakening was more than new rituals; it was an illuminating path, an exuberant outlook of reality and the meaning of life.

Sol's religious transformation made him apprehensive about his recent past. Wasn't being a Stickball star also a worthy goal? Was he going to remain in the crowded tenement on Vyse Avenue for the rest of his life? He also wondered about his mother's parents and family who had remained in Poland. Why had Gittel spoken so little about her early life? He knew even less about the early life of his father. Why had he come to America with his father, Aunt Miriam and Uncle Nuta?

Rabbi Fox inspired Sol and the other pupils of the Hebrew School with a fundamentalist faith: There was a God in Heaven who created every person with a special purpose, and a master plan for the entire world. Though the ultimate plan of God was unknown, the Torah assured us, by the prophets, that there was an accounting for everything that transpires in the world. There was a judgment for every person's acts. God was watching and keeping score and one had to obey and observe the Divine commandments or was punished. However, the observance of the commandments would bring blessedness and happiness. This simple and naïve theology was adequate for Sol - a twelve year old, looking to ground his life with deeper and solid roots. The rabbi showed his humility by speaking personally to them and treating them as friends and buddies rather than pupils.

Rabbi Fox informed the class that an afternoon Hebrew School program was inadequate to appreciate the eternal truths of Torah. Sol would have to transfer to a yeshiva day school with more hours devoted to Torah study to become a "Ben Torah," an authentic Jew. When Sol approached his parents about leaving public school and attending a yeshiva, they felt deeply troubled. All their neighbors sent their children to a public school in the morning and to an afternoon Hebrew School in preparation for Bar Mitzvah. Public schools were necessary for Americanization; yeshivas were antiquated, and Old-World. The decision was held in abeyance for a few months.

The following February, Sol completed sixth grade and graduated P.S. 66 with the highest marks. He anticipated receiving the Roosevelt Medal; but, the coveted award was given to a blonde, Gentile girl from the other sixth grade class. The Principal announced, at the graduation ceremony, that Sol and the recipient were tied for the award; but, upon further deliberation, the girl was chosen. Sol was deeply disappointed; and it wasn't until years later, that he understood the selection -the deference to the Gentile candidate was politic. The principal was Jewish, as were most of the teachers. Were a Jewish student granted the Roosevelt Award, there would be a repercussion, a murmur that the faculty was predisposed towards Jews. Was it not more fitting that the prestigious award be granted to an authentic American pupil, rather than to one of the Jewish children of recent immigrants?

Sol was enrolled in Prospect Junior High School 40, where most of the students were Blacks; unlike P.S. 98 Herman Ridder Junior High School, which was predominantly White, and considered, "safe." Prospect Junior High was the quintessential "Blackboard Jungle." The few Jewish and Italian students were placed in rapid classes with a small number of very bright middle-class Blacks.

It was Sol's first encounter with violence in the schoolyards and in the classrooms. Groups of Black students boasted about their regular trips to the local Five and Ten Cent stores to engage in petty theft, and then to sell the stolen goods in school. Once, a Black student attacked a gym teacher during sessions, and Sol related this to his parents who were dismayed. Another neighbor, Herbie, who lived in Sol's building, related how he had to pay daily protection money. Herbie's father went to the principal and put a stop to this practice. Another time, a student pulled out a barber's razor and slashed another student.

It was also the first time that Sol met a number of upper middle-class Blacks, who dressed well, were very bright, and were in the special Rapids Program. Sol became close friends with Leroy, who was one of the brightest pupils and spoke elegant English. Was he from Jamaica?

Sol's earlier encounters with Blacks were very limited. There was "Whitey," Mr. Matthews, who was the superintendent of an adjacent apartment building on Vyse Avenue. He cast fear in all the youth who attempted to use his own basement as a short cut to West Farms Road where the candy store was located. Very muscular and austere looking, Whitey was very polite and amicable to the adults and he would serve as a defender against the muggers and hoodlums who would foray into Vyse Avenue. Another Black, was Joe, polite and accommodating, who shined shoes on the week-end at the corner of Home Street.

White adults feared Blacks who were moving into the East Bronx from Harlem and believed that they were *trashing* their neighborhood. The increase of Black school-violence cast a shadow on Sol's psyche and he remained fearful of their company. Sol's older brother, Seymour, and sister Elaine, had also suffered the frightening experience of Junior High School 40, with its daily occurrences of violence; but they accepted it as part of the normal life there.

"Be careful and don't argue or get involved with the Negro students," Seymour cautioned. "Also, stay home from school when the classes plan to have a war and, above all, don't look directly into their eyes."

Sol spent six months at Junior High School 40 and related all the unpleasant and horror stories to his parents. But they were still preoccupied with the unfolding tragedy of the Holocaust. To his parents, the word, "horror" meant: pogroms, starvation in ghettoes, systematic shooting, and gas-chambers. What did Sol understand about the real horrors and tragedies of life? Added to Sol's frustration in school, was the fact that many neighbors on his block lied about their address, and were thus able to enroll their children in mostly White schools like P.S. 98 Herman Ridder, and P.S. 75.

Years later, when Sol encountered the highly talented Black basketball players and their sportsmanship, he was able to relinquish his prejudices and have normal relationships with them. Sol would always recall P.S. 40 and the close camaraderie he had with the other White students who gathered together for lunch, and one Black student, Leroy, who was smartly tailored, and very refined.

By June, Gittel and Louis were convinced that Sol would be safer and better off in a yeshiva with its Jewish student body. Sol's parents listened to the Yiddish Radio Station, WEVD, and heard the voice of Rabbi Garfinkel plead for donations for his day school, *Yeshiva Rabbeinu Chaim Ozer*, on Bryant Avenue. He pleaded for funds to cover the many scholarships granted to the poorer students.

"That's the yeshiva for our son," Gittel said to Louis. "Make arrangements for him to get a scholarship." Louis went with Sol to meet Rabbi Garfinkel who was pleased to know that Sol attended Sabbath services regularly, and always donned a cap. A full scholarship was granted. Louis was always sent to plead for a scholarship, rather than Gittel, who was more sophisticated. Louis was sincere and ingenuous, almost child-like, and convinced the principal that he was in need of a scholarship.

Sol was delighted to tell Rabbi Fox that he would attend a yeshiva the following September. His broad, infectious smile noted approval and a sense of accomplishment, in his year's teaching at the Hebrew School. Though Sol's transformation was one of the rabbi's notable achievements, he was disappointed that some of the other bright students would remain in public schools.

In June, Rabbi Fox left the Hebrew School and returned to Brooklyn. Sol lost contact with his rabbi until he met him, years later, in Brooklyn, and reported cheerfully that he was attending a Rabbinical School in the neighborhood.

This transfer to a day school conflicted with his fellowship and camaraderie with the other boys on the block and drew the final curtain on his Stickball career. However, he had a passionate feeling that a more intensive Hebrew education was preparing him for a higher vocation.

IN SEPTEMBER, Sol began attending the yeshiva with longer hours during the week, and on Sundays. The school was located on the top floor of a large, prominent synagogue on Bryant Avenue and 178th Street, near the Bronx Zoo. The seventh and eighth grades were small and combined. Nevertheless, the students were well-behaved and absorbed their lessons. The class environment was warm and cozy, and the teachers were very dedicated. In fact, Sol loved his teachers and the principal for secular studies, Mrs. Mallen, who also served as a teacher.

The first few months at the yeshiva were challenging for Sol. Many of the other students in this all boy's school had attended yeshiva for six years and were far more fluent in Hebrew and knowledge of *Humash*, the Five Books of Moses. In addition, some were children of Orthodox homes, and were more conversant with the customs and rites. Other students attended in order to escape the violence in the public schools.

The classes were small and Sol began to catch up. With his ability of total recall, he soon became on of the top student in his class. The basic course for the Hebrew department was the study of *Humash*, with the translation from the original Hebrew into Yiddish. Sol felt confused and disappointed that the Hebrew text was translated into Yiddish when all the students of the class were English-speaking Americans. Even the rabbi spoke English to the class. Was there a hidden purpose for translating the text into Yiddish which was the language of immigrants? Sol would later realize that his mastery of this immigrant language was essential to continuing in Rabbinical School where the classes were conducted in Yiddish.

It was auspicious that Sol made the acquaintance of the few Orthodox youth who lived in his neighborhood. Jackie Stein, a few years his senior, lived across the street in one of the brownstones, and was attending Yeshiva College. He felt a sense of kinship to Sol in his entrée into Orthodoxy and offered his tutelage. Jackie introduced him to the Young Israel Synagogue, which was attended, mostly, by Sabbath-observant Orthodox Jews. Sol felt comfortable knowing that he was among other youth who also attended yeshivas. The Young Israel was led by a volunteer rabbi and the services were conducted by the laymen - not by a professional cantor. The *shul* was small and informal; people chatted during the services when they weren't singing together. There was no *shenudering* [soliciting donations], when one received an *aliyah,* an honor to be called to the Torah.

Jackie invited Sol to his home on the Sabbath and they began to study together. Jackie was the youngest of four children and his family was strictly Orthodox. His elderly father was diminutive, with a grey goatee, and he radiated wisdom and piety. Jackie guided Sol to the broader world of Orthodoxy, meeting new friends and advocating the ideal that one could be both American and Orthodox. Jackie disabused the stereotype of Orthodox Judaism being Old

World, un-American, and out of tune with modern life. Jackie, too, was cut off from the other Jewish youth on Vyse Avenue who played Stickball on the Sabbath and did not keep Kosher.

IN NOVEMBER, Sol was being prepared for his Bar Mitzvah which required the knowledge of cantillation for the Torah and the additional *Haftorah,* selection from the *Prophets.* After two brief lessons, Sol mastered both, was given a brief Yiddish sermon, and he was prepared to undergo the public acceptance of his adulthood into the Jewish faith. His parents paid the Bar Mitzvah teacher the enormous sum of twenty-five dollars and selected the prestigious Bryant Avenue *shul* for the celebration.

During the morning of his Bar Mitzvah, Sol was apprehensive. He wished he did not have to undergo the public chanting of his portions. But he presented his portions in an admirable manner, and was showered with bags of candy, as was the custom. Following his chanting of the *Haftorah,* he was urged to conduct the *Musaf,* additional prayers, but he felt too uneasy to accept, though he was qualified.

He had acquitted himself as a true yeshiva student, delivering the brief sermon in Yiddish, which deeply impressed both the Lithuanian Rabbi Marcus, and many of the congregants who were immigrants. This was a rare experience for the Bryant Avenue *shul* where most of the Bar Mitzvah boys of the afternoon Hebrew School were neither observant nor participants of the Sabbath services, and could not speak Yiddish.

Vyse Avenue

A Kiddush, collation, was sponsored by the Friedman family for the general congregation, and a separate luncheon was held at their home for the family and relatives. Gittel called on her cousin, Surka, to prepare the cakes. The furniture of the living room was moved to the bedroom, leaving space for two long, rented, tables and chairs, for the thirty guests.

A highlight of the luncheon was the knock on the door and the surprise appearance of Rabbi Marcus. He explained that he had a special affection for Sol who was a regular worshipper at Sabbath services, a yeshiva *bochur,* and had acquitted himself as an authentic Orthodox Jew. Gittel and Louis beheld the Rabbi with awe and invited him to join the luncheon. He was seated at the head of the table, where he greeted the guests in Yiddish and offered the blessing. The presence of the eminent rabbi, with a flowing white beard, dressed in a black caftan, was an indelible memory that Sol would recall for the rest of his life.

A MONTH LATER, Sol saw a movie starring his favorite comedians, Abbott and Costello. In the closing scene, a professional women's basketball team defeated the local collegiate team. Sol felt titillated by the skill of the players, their dribbling, and expert shooting. Basketball, Sol mused, will be my next sport. I'll learn how to shoot and dribble and show those bastards on the Gremlins team that I am not "crap." I've outgrown Stickball on the dirty streets, and fetching the balls from the rooftops of the brownstones on Vyse Avenue. I've outgrown playing *chickie*, rescuing broomsticks, when the cops come around. Basketball appears to be a more pretigious and challenging sport worthy of an athlete.

The culture of Stickball continued on Vyse Avenue for a few more years. Heshy, Duke and Izzie returned from the army. Izzie came home with an injured ankle, but he could still hit spectacularly and play center field. Duke and the other stars started working full-time, married, and moved away. Bones was still a star hitter.

When the war was over, people began buying cars and parking on the street. The streets were too crowded for play, and Stickball had to move to the schoolyards and playgrounds. This was the twilight of the supremacy of Stickball and the luminescence of its former stars.

SOL'S APPRENTICSHIP in basketball was initiated during recess time at the yeshiva. He learned how to dribble and shoot a basketball. But his year in eighth grade also proved fruitful because he learned to master Yiddish, which was necessary for his future schools. This insistence on Yiddish, Sol felt, was symptomatic of a profound disconnect between yeshiva education and American reality.

At the end of the year, Sol graduated as the valedictorian, and passed his entrance test to enter the prestigious Talmudical Academy High School, located in Washington Heights in Manhattan. The imposing structure in Moorish style, built in 1928, included both the high school on the second floor, and the college, on the third floor. On the second floor, the main library housed thousands of scholarly tomes. The main floor included a large study hall, the offices, and an impressive auditorium that seated more than one thousand. The combined student population of high school and college was about three hundred, and constituted a close-knit community that cultivated many enduring friendships.

Sol was deficient in the study of Talmud and was tutored during the summer. Louis and Gittel spent the sum of one hundred dollars for tutoring, though it exhausted almost their entire savings! Sol looked forward to attending High School where basketball was paramount and he would try out for the varsity team.

Sol's first year at Talmudical Academy High School was challenging. Though he had graduated as valedictorian from his Bronx Day School, he was impressed with the erudite freshmen from the Salanter Day School. They had studied Humash and Talmud with Hebrew immersion, and were very advanced. The Talmud instructor, for Sol's freshman year, was born in Israel, and was delighted to speak to the Salanter students in Hebrew and to the rest of the class in Yiddish.

What puzzled Sol was the fact that despite their advanced Hebrew learning, the Salanter group exhibited no admirable religious observance or sense of ethics. Some weren't even *shomer shabbos,* Sabbath observant. Others removed their *kippot*, head coverings, when they were a block away from school, contrary to Orthodox custom. The Salanter group formed a clique, self-proclaimed elite, and elected the class officers. Some of the other students resented their arrogance and clannishness.

Sol found some of his classmates' behavior disappointing as they were very adept in cheating on tests, making cribs, skipping classes, and pushy. When he told this to his mother, she exclaimed, "No doubt these children are from poor Russian families, maybe even Litvaks." Mamma was most prescient about these students when a number of them were later suspended from the high school and from Yeshiva College, for breaking into the teacher's lounge to steal tests. Some of the offenders later became lawyers! Other Salanter alumni had excellent character, gifted minds, and excelled in their professions.

There was a choice of two tracks at the high school. Sol attended the yeshiva track, strictly Talmud, leading to rabbinic ordination. Others attended the Teacher's Institute, which had a broad program including Hebrew literature, Bible and some Talmud. Students in this division tended to be less observant.

Sol was only five foot five, hardly tall enough to make the basketball team. He waited until his sophomore year when he was taller and could be more qualified. A chance meeting with Billy, a basketball star, in the local playground, proved fortuitous. Sol kept passing and setting up Billy to score numerous points and succeed. After the game, Billy brought Sol to a practice session of the varsity. Coach Eisenstein was impressed with Billy's description of Sol's talent. The Coach was pleased with Sol's speed and hustle and accepted him as a member of the varsity.

Sol was ecstatic when he received the blue and white satin uniform. He was now a recognized member of the varsity! This was a momentous step in his life - basketball became the next ambition of his life.

After school hours, Sol ran to the local playground to sharpen his basketball skills, but neglected his academic studies. There, he met Sam, a college student, and expert basketball player, who became his mentor. Sam taught him two important basketball skills - how to make a lay-up and how to box out your opponent under the boards. Sam stressed the idea that most players couldn't make a simple lay-up and this hampered their scoring. The ability to box-out under the boards, would give one an advantage over taller players. Sol mastered these two skills and employed them assiduously during his three years on the varsity.

Gittel was alarmed with Sol's fanatical devotion to basketball. "We send you to a yeshiva so that you should play ball all day? You should pay attention to your studies or you'll end up a bum!" Sol neglected his studies and rarely studied. His marks were below "A," for the first time in his life, but they were high enough to graduate.

Sol excelled in his senior year and was the team's leading scorer with more than 11 points average per game. When playing their arch-rival, Cathedral High School, he scored twenty-two points, breaking a school record. The peak of Sol's basketball career came in the city-wide Yeshiva High School Tournament, when he was high scorer in winning the final contest. Among the hundreds who viewed the thrilling finale, Sol was awarded the trophy for Most Valuable Player.

Sol's parents understood little about basketball and why their son was devoting all his time to it. "You are both immigrants and don't understand how important sports are to me!" he scolded his parents. Sol mused, they still had their heads and hearts in the Old Country where children had to grow up at thirteen, and give up fun and sports. This was his time of youth to spread his wings and blossom as a full person.

They had hoped that he would become a doctor. Why not? Was he not a prodigy in school? But Sol was convinced that he could balance his passion for basketball with his academic studies, and succeed in both. He was mistaken. He graduated with marks, below his potential, though he was awarded with membership in the Arista Society and held some offices in the Student Council.

Sol recalled the celebration of his graduating High School class - a trip to Union City, New Jersey, to watch a burlesque show. He was one of the few who felt this celebration was incongruent, if not reprehensible. Sol was not perfect, and sometimes he deviated from his religious ideals, but he felt this activity had crossed a line.

SOL WAS AWARDED an athletic scholarship to Yeshiva College and told by Coach Solomon to work in the Catskills the following summer. Arrangements were made for him to work in the Evergreen Country Club and to play on the basketball team against some excellent collegiate players. He was one hundred and forty-five pounds and was ordered to put on some weight. His job was to work in the Tea Room, eat loads of cake and be ready for the Yeshiva College team at one hundred and sixty pounds.

For the past four years, Sol was living in a sequestered world of Orthodox Judaism with the study of Talmud. He no longer felt connected to Vyse Avenue and was spiritually a denizen of the land of the Bible and ancient Babylonia. His long hours at school, daily practice of putting on t*efillin,* eating Kosher, Sabbath observance, and attending shul every week, created an insular world.

Vyse Avenue

His only friends were his classmates at the yeshiva. The guys on the block would ask his brother, Seymour, "Whatever happened to Sol? Did he die?" Sol was forgotten by the Gremlins, until one afternoon when Gittel received a surprise phone call from a neighbor. "Mazel Tov! Sol is in the newspapers. It says in headlines on the back sports page of the New York Post, "Friedman Shatters Record." Sol was also surprised, but ecstatic, that the Coach sent in the article about his scoring record with his photo. No other kid on Vyse Avenue – neither, Gremlin or Robin - ever made the sports pages of a city newspaper. Sol was a celebrity, and his family felt proud.

He was certain that his friends, Heshy, Stanley, Billy, and Sam, who were his sports mentors, shared his moment of recognition - and especially Jackie, who was his religious guide.

Sol triumphed over that dark moment, when he was shamefully dismissed from the Gremlins. He had outgrown the Stickball obsession of his childhood, and broadened his athletic horizons. He felt jubilant at the prospect of playing with skilled collegiate players in the Catskills and initiating a new and more luminous chapter in his life.

Charles H. Freundlich

MARVIN

MARVIN, THE THIRD SON of Gittel and Louis, was born on a Saturday, a holy day of prayer, joyous eating, singing and prohibited work. But this created a special dilemma; the *bris,* circumcision, was required to be held exactly eight days later on the following Saturday, and this was a complicated family matter. Was there a *mohel,* a certified expert on circumcision, available in the local neighborhood? Would they have to bring in a mohel from Brooklyn and house him for the week-end? Would their family and friends be able to attend the *bris* on Saturday when all the small businesses were open?

Charles H. Freundlich

When Louis came to the hospital and beheld the tiny, crying baby in Gittel's arms, he felt euphoric. The child would be named after his own father. Yet, he thought to himself, the baby's *bris* on the Sabbath was a mixed blessing. Fortunately for them, Rabbi Shmuel Heller, whose *shtiebel* was across the street, came to the hospital and assured the Friedmans that he would accommodate the *mohel* who was coming in from Brooklyn.

Louis Friedman was a regular Sabbath worshipper at the shtiebel and often donated as much as two dollars when he received an *aliyah* or other honors. Rabbi Heller felt affection towards Louis, and treated him with solicitude, as a personal friend. Louis basked in this aura of importance, a feeling he did not receive from his supervisor at the matzah factory.

But on the High Holidays, the Friedmans chose to worship in the more prestigious Bryant Avenue Synagogue with its excellent cantor and outstanding Lithuanian Rabbi, Eliah Marcus. The shtiebel attracted the less educated, the less affluent, the laborers – the *shneiders and shisters*, the tailors and shoemakers, who spoke poor English. At the prestigious Bryant Avenue Synagogue, even those Polish-born members dared not *daven* with their native Galician accent. *Litvish Yiddish* was not only the standard, but de rigueur among those who deemed themselves more refined. A cantor who chanted Hebrew in the Galician accent was scorned and ridiculed as someone unlearned.

Gittel was an expert in the preparations for the festive refreshments. Cousin Surka was called to make the Strudel and help with the baking of the honey cakes. More than twenty *landsleit* were expected from Brooklyn and

Manhattan to attend the *bris,* and Rabbi Heller, who blessed the child. Gittel was conflicted about selecting the special honors - the godfathers, the *kvater* and the *sandek.* Was it to be Herman, her brother (with whose wife she had not spoken to for more than a year), or was it to be Nuta, Louis' older brother, or Cousin Surka's husband, Ben, who were her closest and most supportive relatives? Thank God, she thought, her brother Herman's wife took sick and the honor went to Nuta.

When Marvin was three years old, he strayed from his sister, Elaine, who was watching him, in front of their house. He fell into a deep construction site in front of their building and fractured his skull, and was in the hospital for two weeks. Gittel feared he was going to die and she wailed and cried with prayers for days: "Was God punishing me for keeping the grocery store open on Shabbos? Maybe I didn't send enough money to my father who was still living in Galicia? Perhaps it was because I haven't spoken to my brother, Herman, and his wife, who had a face like a Pekinese?"

Miraculously, Marvin awoke, came out of the crisis and was completely healed. Gittel kissed Marvin's hands and feet, thanked God, and vowed to give charity every day for the next month. Louis attended *shul* every morning and offered a special blessing, *hagomel,* for his son's recovery; and he sponsored a modest Kiddush the following Sabbath. After the second week, all Marvin could recall was his family waiting around his bed in the hospital and Elaine wearing a plaid skirt.

The accident drew the family together and Elaine had a special relationship with Marvin for years to come. By the time he was four, it was apparent that Marvin had problems with speech. Even Gittel, who loved her son dearly, was beginning to suspect problems. In kindergarten, he played alone, hardly aware of the other children. Mrs. White, his teacher, called Gittel, "Marvin is such a lovely child but he is always by himself, not playing with the other children. I would recommend that he be tested by a professional. The school will pay for the test. He may have a serious problem."

Gittel responded defensively, "I don't understand. Does Marvin cause trouble in class? Does he bother the other children? He is so nice at home. What's the problem?"

"Mrs. Friedman, the purpose of Kindergarten is to socialize the child. I'm afraid that Marvin is a little behind. I feel it is most important that he be tested; and if he has a problem, we can give him attention in a special program."

Marvin scored in the 90's on the Intelligence Test, and was classified as normal. He was not on the level his parents anticipated; nor was he as bright as his older brothers. Their dreams of his going to college, to be a professional, a doctor or lawyer, were shattered. Gittel and Louis were thrown into a state of depression. How could this be? He was such a happy child, with curly blond hair and blue eyes. He smiled often and loved to play with his toys. Gittel hugged him often, held him closely before his bath and exclaimed, "You are my sun, my light, my joy."

Marvin also had difficulty in printing his letters. He not only pronounced an "r" like a "w," but added extra letters to many words. Once, he visited his Aunt Miriam, on Southern Boulevard, and played with her Persian cat which was grey and furry, unlike the alley cats on Vyse Avenue. Marvin exclaimed with surprise, when he came home,

Vyse Avenue

"Mommy, Mommy, the cat has a *fuwel* like a *skwurel*." His brothers teased him about the incident and it troubled him for a long time. Seymour and Sol accompanied him to school every morning and brought him home. They also cautioned him about running into the street.

By third grade, Marvin had developed a strategy for dealing with his slow learning. He became rebellious and refused to do any assignments in class. His teacher, Mrs. Skoval, was losing her patience. She scolded him often, without success, to motivate his interest in class. In desperation, she called on his older brother, Sol, a star pupil in fifth grade, to hear her complaint. Mrs. Skoval brought Marvin to the front of the classroom and exclaimed, "Marvin, why can't you be like your brother Sol who is an 'A' student? I'm sure Sol always follows directions." Marvin grimaced, and then stuck out his tongue, and the class responded with delirious laughter.

From then on, Marvin suspected that Sol was an ally of his nemesis, Mrs. Skoval, and he continued to be defiant. By the end of the term, Gittel noted on his report card: Conduct - D, Effort - D, Arithmetic - A. Try as he might to be disruptive, Marvin always scored high marks in arithmetic which came effortlessly to him. The truth of the matter, Marvin was bored to death, especially with Mrs. Skoval. His lagging social-skills hardly revealed his special aptitude with arithmetic, working with his hands, fixing toys and building objects.

Marvin entered Hebrew School at the Bryant Avenue Synagogue like his older brothers, and was a poor student. He was bored with the useless and irrelevant information about the Jewish past. He wanted to do things with his hands.

By the time he was ten, the consciousness of his forthcoming Bar Mitzvah was causing stressful episodes for him and his family.

Two years earlier, Seymour had presented his blessings before the Torah and the *Haftorah* with great aplomb. Similarly, the Bar mitzvah celebration for Sol, the following year, was most extraordinary and memorable. Sol had already attended a Yeshiva for a year, had mastered the blessings for Bar Mitzvah in two lessons, read from the Torah, and most extraordinary, he delivered a speech in Yiddish.

Now it was Marvin's turn to be a Bar Mitzvah and present his blessings, Biblical portions, and his musical talents, before family and congregation. The very idea overwhelmed Marvin, and made him panicky. He reacted to this crisis not unlike other children. He became taciturn, aloof - and incontinent. Once, when Mrs. Skoval scolded him, he farted, creating a hilarious scene in the class and humiliating his teacher. It was an unforgettable scandal, often recalled by his classmates.

Marvin refused to receive Bar Mitzvah lessons. He was adamant in not wishing to be humiliated before two hundred congregants, family and friends. He had experienced enough degradation and teasing from his brothers, who imitated his baby speech - and enough insults from that *wicked bitch*, Mrs. Skoval, who embarrassed him in front of the class. He had his fill!

Gittel screamed, "You must get Bar Mitzvah lessons, even if I have to drag you to Hebrew School. It's a shame for a Jewish boy not to have a Bar Mitzvah. I'll be ashamed to see my family. *Gevalt* [calamity] - my father in Galicia should not know of such a disgrace from his grandson."

"No, Mamma. I won't go! Even if you kill me, I won't go. I hate Hebrew School!"

"Hate shmate," Gittel countered. "You are going!"

"No, Mamma. You can break my bones, take away my toys, but I won't go."

"I'll take away your erector set."

"I won't go - never!"

Louis intervened, "How about Sol teaching you? He knows all the musical cantillations for *Maftir* and *Haftorah* for the Bar Mitzvah."

Marvin thought for a moment, better Sol than a god-damn Hebrew teacher.

Louis continued, "And after your Bar Mitzvah, you can quit Hebrew school and we'll buy you all the model plane sets you want. You'll receive a lot of money for gifts."

Marvin was silent.

Louis elaborated, "And if you prefer, we can celebrate the Bar Mitzvah at the small *shtiebel* with Rabbi Heller across the street."

"No," replied Marvin. "I'm as good as my brothers. I'll take lessons from Sol and have my Bar Mitzvah at the large Bryant Avenue shul."

"Thank God," murmured Gittel. "We won't be shamed before the family and neighbors."

Sol was patient and taught Marvin the proper notes. After five months Marvin was well-prepared.

On the morning of the Bar Mitzvah, Marvin kept thinking, "Please, God, don't let me pee in my pants."

The family was seated in the front row of the synagogue and they waited with great anticipation for Marvin to be called to the Torah to present his blessings. He chanted his blessings, read from the Torah and his Haftorah with great finesse; and he did not pee in his pants - even when he delivered his three-minute speech.

Louis' face was glowing with joy; Gittel was crying but Elaine, Sol and Seymour applauded. The congregants tossed small paper bags of candy and raisins at Marvin when he concluded his final blessings; and a sigh of relief swept through the family. Sol was invited to conduct the *Musaf*, concluding services, as an honor to his parents, compensating for his refusal at his own Bar Mitzvah.

In the balcony of the synagogue, reserved for the women, there was an uninvited guest viewing the Bar Mitzvah service - Mrs. Skoval. She met Gittel and Louis in the vestry at the Kiddush reception. Mrs. Skoval beamed a smile and said, "I believe the correct Hebrew words are, 'Mazel Tov,' Mrs. Friedman. I am not of the Hebrew faith, but I was interested in Marvin's confirmation. I was most impressed with the services." Then, she turned to Marvin; "Mazel Tov, Marvin, I am so proud of you. Today, you were truly a man."

Marvin's face was blank as he beheld Mrs. Skoval. Gittel was also perplexed, having heard of Marvin's extreme animosity towards his teacher. She responded, "Please, Mrs. Skoval, we would be honored if you would attend the luncheon at our home, only a few blocks away, on Vyse Avenue." Mrs. Skoval smiled and accepted the invitation graciously.

Vyse Avenue

Rabbi Marcus did not attend the luncheon, but the few kind words he offered Marvin and the family at the services, brought them great satisfaction. Rabbi Heller came late to the luncheon and offered some inspiring words of Torah, and congratulations to Marvin and the family. Cousin Surka had made the delicious Strudel and the honey cakes that everyone enjoyed. Uncle Herman offered an envelope with a very generous check, and his wife (with whom Gittel was not amicable) provided a large platter of sweet Gefilte Fish.

During the entire affair, Gittel thought about the missing guests - her family, that remained in Poland, and were murdered by the Nazis. Had she done enough to secure the documentation and the ship tickets to save them? Blima Lipschitz, one of the few survivors of her hometown, attended with her second husband and Gittel felt comforted.

Mrs. Skoval stayed for the whole luncheon and before leaving, she shook Marvin's hand, and said, "I am so proud of you. I knew you would do well." Then she handed Marvin a small package.

After lunch, Marvin opened the package and was astonished. It was a fountain pen - a black Parker 51', with a gold cap. Marvin felt the tears in his eyes.

Charles H. Freundlich

SEYMOUR

SEYMOUR FRIEDMAN WAS unlike the other boys on Vyse Avenue. He grew very tall between the ages of ten and twelve. Like his father, he had blond wavy hair and was often called, "Red," by the other kids on the block. He was a head taller than his classmates, and the tallest student in P.S. 66. This caused him to walk with a slight stoop and his mother, Gittel, feared that he would become a hunchback. She brought him to Dr. Schlain, who diagnosed his condition as mild Kyphosis He recommended a period of physical therapy and exercises, to be held at the hospital and repeated at home. This would remedy the problem.

Gittel mused, what have I done, God, to cause his illness? She took him to the hospital in Manhattan twice a week for extensive physical therapy and exercises; and he repeated these exercises,   three times a week at home. There was slow improvement; but Seymour was not pleased. He viewed himself, a *misfit*.

 Seymour stopped playing with the other kids who, he felt, were talking behind his back about his deformity. His behavior in school became erratic and his marks on his report card indicated failure. He would have to be left back a term and needed remedial help in arithmetic. The other kids teased him and called him, "left-back," and, he ceased to join with them, in his favorite sports, Stickball and Punchball.

Gittel was perplexed by his aberrant behavior at home. He came late for dinner and stayed out late. But despite his behavior, Gittel loved and cared for him. She forced him to do his daily exercises at home, though he resisted; and, she accompanied him, by subway, to the hospital for his therapy.

The ordeal of spending his afternoons at the hospital twice a week diminished his freedom for radio time or camaraderie. The doctor asserted that his rapid growth would slow down, and his abnormal condition would end in a few years. Meanwhile, Seymour had to develop ways of amusing himself alone, to avoid the hurtful barbs from the other kids. He discovered a kindred spirit in another boy, Danny, who was also withdrawn, and used to run for miles in the afternoon. Seymour joined him in his afternoon runs up the length of Vyse Avenue until the Bronx Zoo. This became a daily routine for both of them.

Vyse Avenue

Although, Seymour acquired a reputation as a speedy, long-distance runner, he was still an *outsider* to the other kids who played Stickball. Running long distances gave Seymour a feeling of relief from the ridicule of the other kids. As long as he could run, he felt secure, free and independent. He loved to feel the wind brushing against his face, and could outrun every other kid on the block. He looked forward to high school where they had track teams and awards for champions. Someday, he would receive his due recognition as a star runner.

The isolation from his family and neighbors, infused feelings of anger and fear. He developed pains in his stomach and often had Diarrhea. One afternoon, after dinner, he lost control and defecated in his pants. Marvin smelled the odor and taunted him. Seymour smacked him hard and then rushed to the toilet. Seymour ran out of the house in desperation, swearing that he would have his revenge, and his day of respect. He ran the nine blocks up Vyse Avenue and then walked to the Zoo, planning his strategic comeback.

Gittel and Louis were dumbfounded by Seymour's deep emotional stress, but they concentrated on his physical handicap. Perhaps when he became well, physically, he would become normal, mentally. They were overwhelmed with the basic problems of paying the monthly rent of forty dollars and having enough food on the table. However, they ordered a private telephone and this added to their monthly worries. Seymour's emotional crisis would have to wait until life was more settled.

But Seymour could not wait, nor could he tolerate the present situation. He felt betrayed by his parents' indifference to him. They were more interested in the petty things of daily life, rather than his deep sense of pain. Life was not fair to him. He felt his father, Louis, was a *loser,* hardly able to feed his own family. Were it not for the extra money Gittel earned from knitting sweaters and crocheting doilies, they would have starved.

There was also the rivalry with his brother, Sol, the *perfect goodie*, upon whom his parents lavished much praise for his excellent marks in school. His parents took great pride in Sol's reputation of being the top student at P.S. 66. It was proof that Sol was their favorite. There was also the special attention given to Elaine, *their only daughter*. Once, Mrs. Cohen met Sol in the office, and discussed Seymour's behavior and poor marks. Couldn't Sol help him along?

In Hebrew School, Seymour was disruptive. He joined with Davy, no less a delinquent, and they became the terrors of the student body. But the principal, Rabbi Peskin, was not empowered to expel them. Every dollar in tuition was needed.

When Seymour approached the age of thirteen, he was preparing for his Bar Mitzvah. His private tutor often exclaimed, "Seymour has a cat in his head." Seymour was defiant, and committed to proving them all wrong.

He performed superbly in the Bryant Avenue Synagogue on his Bar Mitzvah day and his critics were defeated. Gittel hugged him with praise. The Friedmans basked in the glory of their oldest son's successful rendition of the prayers. It was Seymour's greatest day and all eyes were filled with joyous acclaim for the thirteen year old who was now six feet tall. He thought, this was my supreme victory - you were all wrong.

His moment of glory was brief; and Seymour began hustling to earn a few dollars to contribute to the family as a man. He applied, successfully, for a route to sell the Bronx Home News. He arose at six-thirty in the morning and completed his work at eight, in time for him to go to school. His contribution of six dollars a week added to his stature as an important member of the family.

Seymour felt a sense of unfairness. Neither Sol nor Marvin had to work because they were too young. This was bull! The real reason was: they should be concentrating on schoolwork and out-side work was too hard for them. And Elaine, the precious, *only daughter*, did not have to contribute to the family. Her earnings as a secretary were put into her personal savings account, (as Gittel explained) so that she would have a dowry to get married.

Seymour was furious. He blasted Gittel, "Who the hell needs a dowry to get married? In America people married for love."

This was proof that his parents were inconsiderate. He commiserated with Danny, his running partner, "My parents hate me. I wish I were not born."

Danny countered, "You only think that way because life is chaotic in your home. My father hardly speaks to me when he comes home at night. When I told him that I was accepted to the Bronx High School of Science, he said nothing. He didn't know how lucky I was to be admitted to the greatest school in the world! I also hope to make the track team." Seymour pondered, perhaps I, too, can make the track team.

Seymour entered James Monroe High School with the great optimism that he would be recognized as a superior

129

runner. He loved the school location, filled with two family red-brick homes and tree-lined streets. It was not crowded like Vyse Avenue. He reflected, this is like Long Island, where the rich Jews were moving. Elaine was, already, in her junior year in Monroe taking a commercial course.

Seymour had no difficulty in making the track team in his freshman year. He was six feet four inches tall and his body was slim, with hardly any symptom of his Kyphosis. His first contest was against Roosevelt High School. He was successful and earned a silver pin. He had come in first, both in the five-hundred meter run, and in the four-man relay race.

At last, he earned the respect that he craved. His grades were modest, "C" average, good enough. No matter, his great passion was running and winning. His brothers boasted with pride to the other kids on Vyse Avenue, "Seymour, their brother, was the star of Monroe's track team." Even his parents took notice that his behavior was less rebellious. Seymour would disprove their former hurtful remarks. He was not a "left back."

He boasted to Danny, "They said I was great in track, faster than a speeding bullet."

"I knew you would be a winner. You were born to be a champion."

"Do you think that I am ready for the basketball squad? I mean, that's where all the prestige and excitement is at school."

"I think you could do anything you want if you try hard enough. You are tall and fast."

Late that afternoon, the kids on Vyse Avenue greeted him as a local hero.

130

Vyse Avenue

That evening, Seymour went to bed exhilarated that he was an athletic star. He thought; track does not have the prestige of basketball. Danny is right. I am tall and fast. I can become a basketball star with some guidance from the coach.

During his second year at Monroe, Mr. Rogoff, the coach of the basketball team, heard about Seymour Friedman, the six foot four runner, who had won numerous awards for the track team. Could he also play basketball? Seymour was invited to the gym during team practice. He could run faster than anyone on the team and was able to leap high with his hand over the rim. No one ever saw a high school player jump that high, holding the ball with one hand. He was like the great George Mikan of the Lakers.

The coach was impressed with Seymour's athletic ability. He was a natural athlete. Not only could he run, but could jump high enough over the basket to rebound. But could he play basketball? The coach said, "Seymour you've got great athletic talent, but basketball requires technique and special skills. Come down to the practice sessions. I'll have Eddie, the assistant coach, work with you. You have great potential. I suggest you put on some pounds. Basketball, unlike track, is a contact sport, especially under the boards."

Seymour was jubilant. Four years earlier, he was doing his exercises for his back; now his back was straight enough for him to compete against the best athletes. The "best" was Clinton High School which Monroe had not defeated in years.

After three weeks of vigorous coaching, Eddie reported to the Coach, "It's no use. This kid is all legs, without the skill to shoot a basket. He jumps high and runs fast, but he's not basketball material."

Seymour received the news with great shock and dismay. I don't understand. I can run and jump. Why won't they take me? They said I was clumsy and couldn't dribble the ball or make an easy lay-up shot. So what! I could learn.

He went to the Coach and pleaded, "Please, give me another chance."

The coach was direct, "Stick to track. That's your sport."

When Seymour met with Danny he cried, "I needed to make the basketball team. The coach doesn't understand."

Danny replied, "The coach knows what he is doing. He's interested in winning games, not being a nice guy."

"But, Danny, you're my best friend. I thought you would understand and support me."

"I am your friend. Your sport is track. You simply are not basketball material."

"Who needs to be a star runner?"

"We can still run together up Vyse Avenue like before. You can be a star in one sport."

THAT EVENING Seymour slept soundly. He began to dream. He could see vividly that he was wearing the Monroe colors and was warming up for the basketball game against Clinton, the undisputed champs of the Bronx. Everyone was looking at him, the tall track star who was now the starting center for Monroe. They were cheering him as he took his warm up shots. He could see the thousands of viewers in the Garden all looking at him - Seymour, the star center -former outsider and misfit, who was excluded from the Stickball games.

The contest of the two Bronx rivals was close and ferocious for three quarters. But near the end of the last quarter, Clinton was ahead by three points. Then, Seymour scored a hook shot. With thirty seconds left in the game, Clinton led by one point.

Monroe had the ball and Coach Rogoff called for a time out and planned the final play. The ball would go from Rothstein to Friedman who was playing the bucket. This was their last chance to tie the score. Then, the coach tapped Seymour on the shoulder and whispered, "When you get the ball, I want you to be deep into the key. Turn and score - we need two points to win this game."

The eleven thousand spectators in Madison Square Garden were silent with apprehension. This was the last play of the game. Rothstein tossed the ball to Seymour who was in the bucket. He was guarded by two Clinton players who pounced on him while he took a hook shot. He missed, but he was fouled, awarding him two free throws. Once again, a deep silence pervaded the Garden.

Seymour breathed heavily; and, successfuly completed the first throw. Tie score! The Garden was in an uproar. He paused, looked back at the coach and felt a sharp sensation in his stomach. Please God, don't let me make in my pants. Then Seymour threw a perfect foul shot. Monroe wins! Monroe wins! The Garden erupted with pandemonium. Delirious screams of victory filled the air as the Monroe players jumped up to hug Seymour. The coach embraced Seymour, "You did it. We knocked the crap out of Clinton!" Seymour mused, thank God, not out of me.

SEMOUR AWOKE the following morning with a broad smile. He thought, "Was it real?"

Gittel entered his room and asked, "What's so funny? Get up. I've made some pancakes for you, my big, beautiful track star."

Seymour was too confused to respond. He mused - I had my greatest victory.

PARADISE GAINED

THE EVERGREEN COUNTRY CLUB, in Fallsburg, New York, was eighty miles from the Bronx. Within five miles, there were more than sixty other resorts known as, *The Borscht Belt*. The clientele was exclusively Jewish, though most of the guests were not religious. They were mostly immigrants from Eastern Europe or first generation Americans and had simple tastes. They knew little about etiquette at the table, but loved to eat, sit on the porch and go for walks after each meal.

The bus bringing Sol to the hotel stopped at Old Falls, with its three stores, Post Office and Night Club, a mile away. When Sol beheld the Evergreen nestled in a lush thicket of trees and manicured lawns, he thought to himself, *this must be Paradise.*

The three buildings of the hotel were ensconced with tall trees. The main building had a wide porch with rocking chairs for people to sit and chat and size up the new arriving guests. This was Sol's first experience away from the city; and the Catskill Mountains with its rustic beauty overwhelmed him, exceeding the tales he heard from some of the neighbors on Vyse Avenue who were regular summer visitors.

Sol Friedman was elated at the prospect of working in the Evergreen Country Club, a prestigious hotel in the Catskills. It would combine fun, earning money, and a feeling of independence. He would have to play on the hotel's basketball team two evenings a week, providing entertainment for the guests. With a flexible schedule, a few nights and a few mornings, he would travel to the other hotels. Basketball was the most exciting family entertainment, and the guests were thrilled to see their waiters playing ball and scoring. The team's players were drawn from various colleges: Yeshiva College, City College and Brandeis. Others were former high school players from DeWitt Clinton, Lincoln and Talmudical Academy.

Sol was jaunty and very aggressive on the court. Less than six feet, and very slim, he could run and out jump much taller players, and had excellent stamina. Now, he would be playing against taller and stronger college players and felt challenged. At one hundred forty-five pounds, he would have difficulty rebounding; and was mindful of the Yeshiva coach's order to gain fifteen pounds during the summer. Sol retained the instruction of Sam regarding blocking-out and lay-ups, which would prepare him against taller and more experienced college players.

The outdoor concrete basketball court was near the swimming pool, which was filled with many chairs and tables surrounded by a four-foot fence. On the side of the basketball court there were long rows of concrete steps that served as seats for the guests. The games were played under the lights when the evenings were cool.

It was an excellent opportunity for Sol to meet new people outside his yeshiva environment, and to grow and develop. Sol worked with two other waiters in the Tea Room located below the Playhouse. His fellow Tea Room waiters were Miki, an immigrant from Hungary and Stanley, a rabbinical student at Yeshiva College. They cooperated in working shifts and pooling their tips. This left an incredible amount of time for Sol to play basketball in the afternoons and evenings.

It was very tempting to eat the rich cakes and cookies that were served (mainly, the leftovers from the previous dinners). Following the evening shows, people would gather in the large Tea Room to socialize. Sol was appalled to see some of the rabbis and guests acting inappropriately, telling off-color jokes, in an atmosphere of levity. But he considered that it was vacation time in the Catskills, far away from the normal, disciplined lifestyle of the city.

On the second day, he met a number of interesting characters. Hy, the Athletic Director, was an army veteran, tall, dark, bronzed, and strikingly handsome. He could have passed for Stewart Granger, and wore a flirtatious smile. He was twenty-four, single and very experienced with women.

Hy prepared the schedule for the basketball team and

accompanied them when they traveled to other hotels. Every morning, he conducted callisthenic classes and *Simon Says* games, after breakfast. When he met the youthful Sol, he smiled and asked, "Have you ever been laid?" Sol laughed, but did not respond. Hy understood that Sol, a yeshiva student, was probably a virgin, and he assured him that he would be his mentor, and would introduce him to the world of love and romance.

Another interesting member of the staff was Mel, the life-guard, who was well-built, blond, blue-eyed and in his twenties. Like Hy, he radiated a sophistication that impressed Sol. The third member of the athletic staff, Sy, was tall, and very muscular, and crude in his demeanor, but very spirited. The athletic staff worked together and was expected to socialize and entertain the guests at the Playhouse in the evening. They did more than simply *entertain* the guests.

The hotel staff lived in an old wooden cottage. It was probably the original hotel, with ten rooms, no locks on the doors, no ceilings under the roof and double-decker bunk-beds. Thus, it was always noisy and lacked privacy. The life-style was casual and the staff borrowed books and personal items from one another. A few of the staff, like Hy, had their own cars and invited the others to join them when they drove to town.

This was Sol's first experience in group living and he adjusted well. He felt he was part of a close and friendly community, where there were no parents setting standards; but older coworkers, who could mentor him in the realities of life. He felt liberated from the strictures of his parents, free to be authentic, and do what he felt in his heart. He felt grown-up and responsible for his own life.

The auxiliary Tea Room, in the Main Building, opened at 7:00 A.M. to accommodate the men who attended early minyan, and also, for those who were unable to sleep. Sol had the morning shift from 7:00 A.M until 8:30 A.M., when the Dining Room opened; and, he was free for the rest of the morning. He liked to mingle with Hy, who told him about his adventures in the army, and especially his experiences with women. He was shocked to hear that Hy was intimate with one of the female staff who was a graduate of a Beth Jacob Orthodox school!

The Evergreen Country Club attracted the affluent, modern-Orthodox community and others who wanted to keep Kosher, but conducted an un-Orthodox life style. Morris Levy established the hotel thirty years earlier, with his wife, Molly, and it was now run by his two sons. After Morris died, Molly was the titular head and was ever present in the kitchen with a fly swatter. She made sure the food was not infested and that no one was stealing onion rolls and bagels.

The guests drove up in their Cadillacs and usually stayed for two weeks. A few, like the highly successful Miller family, stayed for the whole summer; and they were given VIP treatment. Their daughter, Ellen, a high school senior, was attracted to Sol and invited him to spend time with her at the pool.

Sol had dated before and was happy to meet new girls, but his experiences never went beyond placing his arm around a girl's shoulder in the movies and a brief kiss on the cheek. Yeshiva students were taught to be modest and to inhibit their sexual feelings. Ellen was pretty and spoke softly. Sol was diffident in her presence. She was the daughter of *Miller's Lingerie*, a well- known establishment on the Lower East Side of Manhattan. She sat close to Sol at the pool and she touched his hand.

"What do you do when you are not a busboy? Ellen asked.

"I'm a waiter, not a busboy, and I plan to attend college as a pre-med student."

"That's wonderful. My brother, Joe, will also be a pre-med student. You must know Joe, from the Mesivta basketball team."

Sol knew him, a tall center for Mesivta, which his team defeated twice during the season.

"Are you free this evening? I mean, do you have to work in the Tea Room? If you're free, Pop said you can have dinner with us."

Sol was flattered, but he knew the hotel rule: No eating with the guests in the Dining Room (but fraternizing with them in the Playhouse was encouraged).

"We could spend some time together after the show this evening, if that's all right with you, and with your parents," Sol responded.

"Pop lets me do anything I want during the summer; he trusts me."

That afternoon, Sol met with Hy and told him about his date with Ellen. Hy cautioned him, "That kid has been here for three seasons with her family. She's smart and fast. You can go so far but be careful not to get into bed with her. Her father will have your ass, if you do."

That evening, Sol shined his shoes, wore a white shirt with a striped tie and a dark sport coat. He met Ellen at the Playhouse. It was filled with guests who listened with great gusto to the Black comedian who rattled off many jokes in

Yiddish. He was followed by a young singer, a refugee from Poland, who sang classic Yiddish melodies. Sol was fascinated by the young singer, a Holocaust survivor, who spoke Yiddish to his audience.

In Sol's experience, only older people spoke Yiddish. It was his first encounter with the new Jewish immigrants whose families were murdered, had survived forced labor camps, and were called "refugees." His mother often spoke about the refugees who had moved to Vyse Avenue. Gittel was friendly to those who moved into their apartment building and even baked cakes for their children. Many of the other Jewish neighbors felt they had a special obligation to help the recent immigrants, forgetting that they, too, were once *refugees.*

Sol and Ellen were not thrilled to be in the Playhouse, filled with old people. "Let's go for a walk where we can be alone," Ellen suggested.

They walked through the great lawn and stopped at the edge of a few trees behind the main building. Ellen pulled Sol to her. Sol was taken by surprise. Dare he kiss her?

"What's the matter?" she asked. "Here, you can hold me."

Sol carefully placed his hand around her shoulder and kissed her on the cheek, and said, "I think we should get back to the Playhouse. You father will wonder where you are."

They meandered, holding hands, and Ellen said, "Will I see you again? I like you a lot."

"I think so. But I'm here to work, earn some money and play basketball. I'll be around the whole summer."

Sol led a sheltered life, shaped by his Orthodox yeshiva values. This was a romantic encounter, something

141

new; and he felt exhilarated, but conflicted. He would be experiencing a complicated and adventurous summer.

For the next five days, they saw each other often and people thought they were going steady. Mr. Miller was delighted that his daughter was having a happy social life, and approved of Sol - a refined Jewish boy. They had gone beyond simple kissing; but, Sol stopped, and drew a line when she invited him to her room when her parents were out. By the second week, Sol decided to break off with Ellen. He was uncomfortable with her and her sexual desires. Sol had drawn a line and would be faithful to his values.

He still wanted to spread his wings and meet new girls and deepen his relationship with the older staff, Hy, Mel and Sy. He admired them for their urbanity and sophistication, especially with love and romance.

Hy was the radiant star of the hotel and the owners were delighted that he socialized with many of the guests. He was also adept in dealing with difficult situations. Once, during half-time in a basketball game, Hy attempted to demonstrate his skills before the three hundred guests. He dribbled the basketball for the length of the court and just as he was about to shoot, he slipped, and fell on his behind. The crowd roared with laughter. Hy got up from the floor and bowed. The crowd applauded with approval. This was Hy's victory over a humiliating blunder.

One evening, Sol entered Hy's bunk and found him reading a book. Hy boasted, "This book, *One Hundred Novels*, is terrific."

"What's so great about the book?"

"Don't you understand? You read this book which summarizes the whole novel in two pages. Then you can speak about these one hundred great books as if you read them. People then think you're literary, cultivated, and intellectual." Sol was amused by Hy's sophisticated advice.

On another evening, while Sol and his three room mates were asleep, Hy burst in. It was past 1:00 A.M, and he was grinning, holding a young girl around his arms.

"Meet Sally. She's a whore from town. I paid her and she's willing to go to bed with all four of you." Hy held a small packet of condoms in his hand and said, "Hurry out of bed. Tonight you won't be virgins. We'll meet in my bunk."

Sol was perturbed. The thought of sex with a whore was beyond the ken of his plans. But Arthur, his roommate, a third year rabbinical student at Yeshiva College cried out, "Let me go first." Sol refused to leave his bed and could hear the commotion in Hy's room next to his, and the sound of shaking beds on the wooden floor. He found sleeping impossible the rest of the evening; but he was glad he did not go with the others. It seemed unrefined and profane to be sleeping with a prostitute, giving one's body and love to a stranger.

The following Tuesday, the Evergreen basketball team defeated The Fallsview and Sol scored sixteen points. He basked in the applause of the guests and felt taller and more significant. He was thrilled to be playing against two all-American stars from N.Y.U. On Thursdays, the team traveled to other hotels: Brown's, The Pines, and Brickman's. Sol continued to score in double digits.

He began putting on weight by eating the rich cakes in the Tea Room. He enjoyed working with the other waiters in the Tea Room, Stanley and Miki, with whom he shared the tips at the end of the week. They respected his flexible schedule to be free evenings to play basketball, and they scheduled him for the early morning shift.

One unusual event took place on *Tisha B'Av*, a fast day, commemorating the destruction of the Jerusalem Temples. Sol had expected the dining room to be closed. The Orthodox clientele would be embarrassed to be seen eating. Having skipped breakfast, most of the guests showed up for an extravagant luncheon, fit for an epicure, scheduled after the mid-day prayers. Fancy layer cakes and ice cream were served. Sol believed that the guests were motivated by the hedonistic tone in the hotel and the idea that they had already paid for the meals. He was flabbergasted upon viewing the self-indulgence of people who presumed to be Orthodox, yet lived a self-indulgent lifestyle in the hotel. He wondered - does religion also take a vacation?

On Sundays, he called home to tell his Mom and Dad that he was feeling fine and making a lot of money; enough to pay for his clothes and his school tuition. He also sent home some colorful post-cards. He then wrote a lengthy letter to his friend, Sid, who lived on Vyse Avenue:

Dear Sid,

Let me begin by telling you that this has been the most fabulous four weeks of my life. The food is great, the work is easy and there are plenty of women. Working in the Catskills is like living in Paradise. The trees, the flowers and the lawns are gorgeous. You have entertainment every night and there is plenty of time to swim and play ball. I've met a number of interesting people, older than me, especially the athletic director who is very experienced. Being on the basketball team, I don't have to work in the dining room. The guys in the dining room tell me that they work their asses off, but they need the money to pay for college. You know, I'll make more than six hundred dollars for the summer, more than my father. I've been playing on the Evergreen basketball team, have met a few famous college stars, and have really improved. The hotel owners appreciate and respect me.

One thing that's not so hot is the manners of the guests. They eat like pigs and have little refinement. They send their waiters back to the kitchen for an extra piece of butter. There's one nutty woman who insists on a large, fresh salad for breakfast. Another *nudnik* wants his orange juice freshly squeezed - anything to make the staff run around and sweat. You'd think that these guests, immigrants who hardly speak English, came from royalty.

Evergreen is a very nice place, not quite Grossinger's. The entertainment is mostly okay, but sometimes, it's very corny, catering to the immigrants. I often wonder - how come some of these guests who aren't educated, have made enough dough to afford a two-week vacation? We live in a strange world. The dummies are rich, while the teachers are poor.

My social life is great and I've had many romantic encounters - I'll divulge them personally, when I get home. How are things in the Bronx? Is the weather hot? Do you get to Orchard Beach or are you going to Coney Island? Are the guys - Red, Bones and Screw, still playing Stickball or are they gone for the summer? See you when I come home in a few weeks, Regards to the boys.

Your friend, Sol

Charles H. Freundlich

ONE OF THE HIGHLIGHTS of the season was the lavish campfire for the staff, which the owners sponsored with appetizing food, barbecue, and liquor. The evening was cool and many of the boys sat with their arms around girls. Members of the band sang songs and they all felt like one great family. Sol reflected about his relationship with other staff members who were not Orthodox or Jewish. Hy was standing with an attractive red-head sitting on his shoulders, when the photographer snapped a group picture. Hy turned to Sol and asked his persistent question, "Are you still a virgin?" The owners were in the background and Sol was sitting to the left next to Ellen. Pincus, the captain of the waiters, was on the right side.

Sol could never fathom why Pincus, in his thirties, an ordained rabbi from a fine rabbinical family, was not married. Why had he chosen to be a professional waiter, with summers in the Catskills, and winters in Miami? The college students did not consider themselves, *waiters,* but temporary summer employees.

The most memorable person that Sol befriended was Hy, whose singular interest was women. What did he do when the summer was over? Mel, the blonde, handsome lifeguard might well have become a doctor or lawyer. Sol idolized Hy who could have become a Hollywood star. He undoubtedly must have filled his life with more serious matters than chasing women.

The staff campfire, at the end of the season, caused Sol to ponder the meaning of his summer experience. He enjoyed working with the staff, was accepted by them, yet, he felt - he was not one of them. It was apparent that the hotel experience for many of the guests was not reality, but

146

an escape, to live the fantasies, and broken dreams of a dismal life.

For Sol, the tall towering trees and the waterfalls were an Elysian world compared to the lackluster dwellings on Vyse Avenue. Soon he would bid farewell to the Evergreen, and to the care-free, pleasure-seeking world that it exemplified.

Sol had learned to embrace the Catskills and the informal life style. He bid goodbye to Hy, and the rest of the staff, who had become his personal friends. When Sol left Hy, he was sorrowful. Would he ever see the staff members, or hear from them, when they returned to their homes and college campuses, scattered along the eastern seaboard? Sol felt desolate in having to sever his contact with the many interesting personalities he met. Was this all a dream from which he must be awakened?

WHEN HE RETURNED home to Vyse Avenue, he felt the unconditional warmth and love from his parents, Gittel and Louis, and the   friendly and competitive love of Seymour, and Marvin. Gittel and Louis both wept with joy when they saw him.

Gittel remarked, "You've become fat like me."

"Seventeen pounds from the cake, "Sol said with joy.

It would enable him to compete against heavier opponents in his college basketball career. How wonderful it felt to be kissed and hugged by his parents, not for what he had achieved, but for what he was.

Sol felt the dimming of the glow from living in the Catskill Shangri-La; and he discerned the garbage on the streets and the dreary brick apartment buildings that lined

Vyse Avenue. He had experienced an alternate world, had matured, and was prepared to move on to a new chapter.

THE FOLLOWING THREE SUMMERS, Sol worked in other hotels: Grossingers, the Concord and Swan Lake and was able to pay for his clothes, personal expenses and college tuition. Fifteen years later, he returned to the Evergreen with his wife, for a week's vacation. The hotel's main building had been renovated and there was central air-conditioning. The clientele had changed and Chinese and Italian food was on the menu. The basketball court was still in good condition but there were no basketball games for entertainment. The scandals at City College and L.I.U., in 1951, produced a finale to a tradition of basketball entertainment.

Sol lost contact with his hotel friends within a few years. The world of the Catskills was gone within thirty years. The hotels closed or went bankrupt. Younger people chose to fly or take cruises. Hassidim, with their large families, purchased many bungalow colonies and changed the complexion of the Catskills.

Gone were the immigrants who loved the six-course epicurean breakfasts, who could enjoy the rustic scenery, the cool evenings, sitting on the porch and the nostalgic Yiddish jokes and songs. For them, this was Paradise - a world apart from the garment industry, the small shops, the groceries, and the candy stores, where they earned their livelihoods. It was a special world where they could be among fellow immigrants, speak Yiddish, eat gourmet, kosher food, and feel at home. For a few weeks, each guest felt privileged, far from the tawdry atmosphere of Brooklyn and the Bronx.

Vyse Avenue

One of Sol's associates in the Tea Room became an eminent rabbi in Colorado. Another waiter became an outstanding cantor in the South. At least three waiters became doctors. Pincus, the captain of the waiters, remained a professional waiter. Sol realized, once again, while working in the hotel that brains and talent are not enough; the pathway to happiness and success is sacrifice, service and personal relationships.

Charles H. Freundlich

ELAINE

THE FRIEDMAN'S only daughter, Elaine, was especially close to her father who called her, *Mamtsu*. She was twenty-two, and all her girlfriends were either going steady or were married. "What is wrong with me?" She pondered. "I am pretty and intelligent, but I don't attract any boys." She looked into the mirror in the bathroom and saw a plaintive face looking back at her.

The Friedman apartment on Vyse Avenue was commodious and neatly furnished. When an occasional date arrived, he was impressed. Elaine graduated from James Monroe High School with excellent marks and her Commercial Diploma opened up numerous job opportunities for book-keeping and stenography. Her job was steady; she was earning more than her father, and contributed to the monthly household expenses. She worked at Stern's in Manhattan's business district and often ate lunch at Kresgee's.

She loved her three years at James Monroe High School, where she made many friends, and enjoyed walking through the tree-lined streets that surrounded the school. The campus of the school was well-managed. She felt cheerful by the sense of spaciousness, as she walked the mile from her crowded apartment house on Vyse Avenue. She reflected, someday, when I'm married, I'll move to Pelham Parkway or Long Island and have my own home with a front lawn and backyard.

She considered going to college during the day, but Gittel told her that the family needed her financial help. She attended the evening program at City College; and took courses twice a week, while working during the day. She mused, why do I need a college degree? I'm a woman planning to marry and my husband will support me. Men needed college degrees - not women. At five foot three, slender and blonde, I am sure to attract a fine young man from the block.

But her mother cautioned her, "The boys on Vyse Avenue are bums, common, not serious, and not professionals. You could do better. You are beautiful and very cultured. You read books and subscribe to the Ballet season at the City Center. You are more refined than the boys who hang out at the candy store."

Elaine knew, deep in her heart, that those *street bums* weren't interested in her. They used to call her, "vinegar puss," because she grimaced when they made passes at her or whistled. She was jealous of Barbara, who lived in the next building and was always surrounded by boys. Barbara came from a large poor family and her father always sat in front of the building   drinking a bottle of Pepsi Cola.

Hank Moskowitz, who lived in her building, was different, and asked her out more than once. He completed high school before serving in the army in Europe, and was sent home after a bullet pierced his right knee and left him with a slight limp. Elaine didn't mind his handicap. He was kind and soft-spoken, tall, with dark hair. He had a steady job working with his father on a truck that delivered seltzer in the neighborhood. Elaine respected him because he never used curse words or made mention of her body. He made her feel good about herself. He was very devoted to his parents, and like her, he helped out in the house. They shared so much in common, especially the movies and novels.

But, Elaine's mother did not approve. A *shande* [shame], Gittel said. "You would go with a boy whose father is a *balegola,* a truck driver? My family would never marry into such common people. You would be better off marrying into a family of business people."

Elaine was exasperated. She loved her parents, Gittel and Louis, and would never hurt them. She knew how hard they worked in the grocery store, fourteen hours a day. Then, when they lost the grocery store, Louis took odd jobs working with his hands.

Once, he took a well-paying job in a liquor store in Yorkville. He had to lift the cartons of liquor and do heavy work. Louis knew how to take orders and never complained.

153

Gittel was surprised when he got the job in Yorkville, which was known to harbor the most anti-Semitic German elements - many who belonged to the Bund. Louis explained that he spoke to the boss in German and they liked him. One day, Louis asked the boss to have time off for the coming Jewish High Holidays, and he was instantly fired. Gittel screamed, "You fool, they hired you because you passed as a German. Why didn't you tell them that your wife was sick?" Louis was incensed. He was too decent to deny his Jewishness, though technically, he was of Austrian nationality.

Elaine was nurtured in guilt and was constantly reminded of her parents' sacrifice for her and her brothers. She could never offend them. It seemed that every boy that she met was not good enough for Gittel, who reminded her that her family in Galicia, the Rudnicks, had status and property. Louis kept silent. He loved Elaine, his first-born, named after his mother, and supported her completely. "Whatever makes you happy is all right with me."

Then there was Benny Shapiro, who was attending City College with the aid of the G.I. Bill of Rights. He was nice looking, finely tailored, and was congenial. Everyone on the block liked him. But Gittel reminded Elaine that Benny's parents were Litvaks. "We never inter-married with them," she asserted.

Elaine reached her limit of tolerance. Did she, at twenty-two, need the approval of her mother? She was an adult, a high school graduate, and was working full-time. She decided that the next boy she liked, she would marry quickly, and run away from home - far from Gittel and her narrow and snobbish attitudes that should have been left in Galicia. This was America - all people were equal.

Elaine understood why she was not as popular as Ruthie and Barbara, who always seemed to be holding hands with the guys who hung out in the corner candy store. She reflected that it was because they let the boys kiss them and even touch their breasts when they were in the balcony of the movie theaters. She was not like them. She was pure, and would save her virginity for her future husband, a fine and educated professional, who respected her mind and character, not just her body.

Elaine was fastidious with her appearance. She wore fashionable dresses to work which she bought at Alexander's, styled her hair, and wore three inch heels. At Sterns, where she worked, some of the men complimented her on her looks; but they were mostly married. Once, she went to a dance at the Starlight Ballroom, next to the RKO Chester, with her best friend, Louise, from Monroe High School. She liked to dance, especially to lively, Latin music, like the Mambo and the Cha-Cha.

The ballroom was filled with single men; some were smoking, others were drinking liquor from their small metal containers. She had no luck. Boys liked dancing with her but they did not take her phone number. Louise, met a nice guy there and became engaged, and this added to Elaine's sense of gloom.

Gittel proposed seeking out a marriage broker who advertised in the Forward. "Mamma, please, no! I can find my own husband. We don't do those things in America!"

Gittel countered, "How do you think I met your father, Louis? And did I do so badly?"

"Mamma, please, no. I want to love my future husband, not buy him!"

Then Elaine met Maurice Klein, at the engagement party for her girlfriend, Louise. He was fashionably dressed, soft-spoken, with a slight foreign accent. She told her mother that he worked in mid-town in a large bank.

"*A banker,*" Gittel smiled with approval.

"And he comes from a fine family," Elaine continued. "Maurice is fair, with thick, wavy hair, and wears expensive suits. His parents are from Budapest." The Friedmans were excited,"A son-in-law from Budapest, the center of culture of the Austrian-Hungary Empire!" Maurice had the endorsement of Elaine's parents.

After two months of dating, Elaine felt sure that she had met her future husband. Gittel invited Maurice's parents to their apartment for dinner on a Sunday evening. The Kleins, from Budapest, were very gracious, refined and stylish in their dress, though they hardly spoke Yiddish. But they spoke Hungarian and German, which impressed both Gittel and Louis, who spoke German with them. Despite the Holocaust, Elaine's parents remained emotionally attached to Germany and Austria which were the pinnacles of Western Culture,   superior to America (though they never voiced it publicly). Both sets of parents heartily consented to the marriage and they agreed to a Sunday afternoon in June, in a catering hall in The Bronx.

Two weeks before the marriage, Maurice met with Elaine at her home, to review all the details of their marriage and their honeymoon. They agreed that right after the marriage ceremony, they would drive to the Catskills for a one-week stay at the *Nevele Country Club*. Elaine and Maurice felt passionate about each other; and they looked forward to their new life together. They rented an apartment in Forest Hills, not far from the subway, and they both would commute to work.

Elaine said, "I would like a baby and would probably stop work after a few months." Maurice was surprised.

"A baby is wonderful. But I thought we would save for a few years and buy a home on the Island; we could have a baby then. Let's wait a few years."

"Why wait? I've saved more than nine hundred dollars. I hate working at Stern's, taking orders and snotty remarks from my supervisor. I've dreamed of marriage and a home of my own and, especially, my own children. Darling let's live now."

"Nine hundred dollars - I thought you had more savings! Darling, I earn fifty dollars a week. With our rent and my car payments we can't afford to live on my salary alone and have children. Bank messengers don't make that much money. A baby will have to wait. If we want our dream home on the Island; you will have to work a few more years. We'll live on my salary and bank your salary."

"I'm twenty-three and I'm tired of the cramped apartment in the Bronx, living with my parents and brothers. I thought you earned more than fifty a week. You dress so elegantly and drive a new Chevrolet."

"I didn't think my salary was that important to you? I make a living. That's all."

"But those restaurants we went to after the movies."

"I wanted to make a good impression."

"But you said you worked in a bank. I thought you were an executive in charge of loans or mortgages - not a messenger boy! Remember, how you told me that we would have a new and beautiful life together."

157

Elaine cried and bit her lip.

"I'm sorry that I gave you the wrong impression. I work for a bank, but I am not a banker."

"I don't understand. I only wanted what every decent girl wants - a family, a child and a husband who supports her. Is my money that important to you?"

"I'm shocked! You're not the Elaine with whom I planned to share a life. No! Children will have to wait - I don't want to be stuck in an apartment in Queens."

Elaine took off her engagement ring. "I'm sorry. I always wanted children and a family of my own. I don't care if we have to live in an apartment, as long as we have children, I would be happy."

"An apartment in Queens is not my idea of a future. I'm glad that we had this talk. Maybe we should delay our marriage."

"That's not necessary," Elaine said. "I'm calling it off."

"But you promised me. You said you have savings!"

For three days, Gittel and Louis tried to encourage Elaine to go on with the marriage. Mr. Klein spoke to his son, "Compromise. Young, newly-weds always argue. Then later, they get used to each other, and love gets stronger."

Elaine felt that her dream was a balloon that burst. She was through with Maurice. Banker indeed! I'm through with boys and their false promises and their shiny cars and elegant suits. I won't get married!

One sunny afternoon, Gittel was sitting in the window when she noticed a man wearing a tan suit, short and stocky, getting out of his blue and white Buick, and parking in front of her building. As he entered her apartment building, Gittel wondered, was this the brother of Marsha, who lived above them on the first floor, and whose maiden name was also Friedman? Marsha had said that he was thirty - seven and not married. She let him sleep over in her apartment on Sunday evenings before returning to his home, in Jersey, the following morning. The following three Sundays, the same man in the Buick returned and entered the building.

Marsha heard about Elaine's break - up and spoke to Gittel about her brother, Max. He had come with his mother from Hungary, years earlier, to join his father, who settled in Jersey. Marsha told Gittel about Max and his successful General Store. The Gentiles in the small farming town in Jersey loved Max and the way he did business - even though he was a Jew. He trusted his customers and they could buy anything - jewelry or appliances, on credit, and paying as little as two dollars a week.

Gittel understood what was on Marsha's mind. Could Max call on Elaine? Gittel mused, Max was an immigrant but he had been in America for sixteen years and could speak English, and made a good living. Gittel was agreeable. True, Elaine was miserable and frustrated with American boys, but Max was more Old Country, settled and serious about marriage.

Elaine came to the window and watched Max as he parked his car. He looked tired, was short, and his suit was not stylish.

"What, old? He's only thirty-seven," said Gittel. "He's mature and well established in business. Marsha says that he owns the property of his store."

Max was not attractive. His hairline was receding and his gait was that of a middle-aged man. Elaine wondered, how can I love such a man? He looks like my father, a typical European immigrant.

"Why not go out with him?" argued Gittel. "Maybe you'll like him. So, he's not so tall and skinny. But he's a serious man and comes from a respectable Hungarian family."

Elaine had not gone out socially since her break-up with Maurice. She had no expectations for being called for a date. When Max called, she thought, "Why not? Max is better than nothing."

Max Friedman was down-to-earth, a realist, and a man of experience. For ten years, he was the man of the house taking care of his mother and younger brother and sister. When he came to America, he was an experienced shopkeeper and jeweler, and was financially independent. He established his own store and did not join with his father in the furniture business. He had no close friends; and trusted no one but his mother. He was independent and a loner. But he knew how to handle customers. He was very affable, making them feel welcome, and they trusted him.

He took Elaine to the Loew's Paradise on the Concourse and then to Krum's ice cream parlor where they chatted for more than an hour. He held her hand, but he did not kiss her good night. He asked if he could see her again the following Sunday when he closed his store. Why not? Elaine reflected. He's better than nothing.

The following week they went to the Lower East Side and dined at an expensive, kosher restaurant. During dinner, Max told her the story of his life, his struggles in a small town in Hungary, when his father immigrated to America leaving him to head the family. For ten years they waited until they were sent tickets to come to America. Max was not drafted into the U.S. military, because he had flat feet. But he was healthy, he assured Elaine, and would continue to work hard to support his wife and children. He was ready to get married.

In the following weeks, Elaine noticed that Max seemed taller. He wore Adler elevator shoes, he explained, and the gray along his side-burns disappeared, thanks to his barber. Elaine tried to speak about her own interests in the Ballet and current novels she was reading. But she saw that Max was indifferent. She realized that Max was like her father, with a limited cultural background, but strong traditional Jewish family values.

"We keep Kosher in our home, "Elaine said. "My mother lights candles every Friday night."

Max was delighted. "I would want my own home to be Kosher just like my parents and their parents."

"What about children?" Elaine questioned.

"I love children. I am one of five."

Max told her that he liked her very much. Could she come to Jersey to meet his mother and brothers? Elaine would discuss it with her parents.

"What do you think, Elaine? Is he your *bashert*, the one God has chosen for you?" asked Gittel.

"He's very nice and kind. He treats me like a lady. He wants me to come to meet his mother in Jersey," Elaine added.

"That's a good sign." Gittel replied. "He respects his mother and wants her approval. That's the way fine people did things in the Old Country."

The following week, Max came to the Bronx and had lunch with Elaine's family. Then they went to Jersey. Elaine

161

would sleep over at a Motel and spend the following day touring the town, its synagogue, and its places of interest.

Mrs. Esther Friedman was delighted that Max had brought home a fine American girl with an education and who kept Kosher. She heartily approved of his choice. But privately, she informed Max - Elaine's nose was rather large.

"Don't worry, Mamma, we can have it shortened with plastic surgery."

Esther Friedman called Gittel to wish her Mazel Tov. Elaine had accepted the beautiful one caret diamond ring.

Their marriage was scheduled for July in the Bronx. Elaine paid the nine hundred dollars for the catered meal; and Max covered the flowers, band, liquor and photographer as was the custom. In addition to Rabbi Perlman of Galicia, Esther Friedman had her rabbi from Hungary officiate. Max paid both rabbis generously.

However Gittel was disappointed. "Such a wealthy man and he asks us to cover the cost of the meal? Was he cheap, or just a shrewd businessman?"

One incident during the wedding revealed Max's strong character. Max began taking movies and was immediately confronted by the caterer, "Sir, this is a union shop. Only a professional photographer, who is a union member, can take movies or photos."

Max responded, "This is my wedding. I demand to take photos!"

"Sir, this is a union shop!"

Max was intransigent, "Sir, this is my wedding!"

"Sir, if you don't stop taking movies, the waiters will not serve the meal. They are all union members."

"Sir, if you don't serve the dinner, I won't pay you. This is my wedding and my money. If you don't like it, you can kiss mine."

"We'll see. Nobody can break the union rules in this catering hall."

Elaine was startled. "What's happening, Max? Will they go on strike?"

Max whispered, "In five minutes you'll see."

Three minutes later, the caterer returned to the dining hall and the waiters began serving the meal. Max continued taking movies. Elaine was impressed. Max was usually easy-going and gentle - but, he was also principled and steadfast, and not a pushover.

ELAINE ENJOYED the pace of small - town life in Jersey. People were more courteous in the stores, less pushy than in New York. Her husband worked long hours in the store and she was soon pregnant with her first child. Max was dependable and considerate to her, especially in furnishing their new split-level, three-bedroom home, almost three-thousand square feet (according to Max's specifications). She adored the large family room and, on a lower level, a laundry room with her own washer and dryer. She loved her commodious home, her French-Provincial Dining Room suite, and plush carpeting. How thrilling it was when Mamma and Daddy visited and marveled at such luxury! What a far cry from their apartment on Vyse Avenue.

When she shopped, she could buy all she wanted, without considering price. This was not Jennings Street. Max taught her how to drive a car and she felt very independent and classy.

But Max was meticulous. The home had to be kept immaculately clean; no dust on the furniture, and dinner was served at 6:00 P.M. sharp. When Max came home from work, the food was to be on the table, warm and ready, beginning with a vegetable soup. Mother Esther was a daily presence ensuring that her son's wife, the American, learned how to cook the Hungarian way. Elaine was to be respectful and accommodating to her husband, like Esther was to her Hungarian husband.

Elaine reflected: Max was plain and uncomplicated. He relished the same soup and main dishes, and didn't complain about the monotony. Every evening he prepared his tuna fish sandwich for lunch the following day. Every evening at eight sharp, he had a large scoop of chocolate-chip ice cream. He lived by a strict regimen. Changes made him feel uncomfortable.

Elaine learned to love Max by the second year of her marriage. She dreaded the very idea of remaining single, an old maid. The security and care that Max provided her was a grand blessing. Her joyfulness in marriage exceeded her expectation of "better than nothing." She realized that Max, in his own way, loved her; although, he was at a loss of words to express it. Elaine chose his suits and encouraged him to go on a vacation at least once a year. He refused saying,"I have my *Gan Eden,* here in my home."

However, in the summer, he drove to the Catskills to bring his mother to her annual two-week vacation at the Evergreen Country Club. Even Max's mother came to accept Elaine as a daughter; especially after her nose was cosmetically improved by an eminent plastic surgeon on Park

Avenue. Their first child, a boy, was named after Max's father, and Esther was overjoyed.

Gittel and Louis admired Max because they had much in common. They spoke the same Yiddish dialect or accented English and shared the same Jewish family values. They were thankful that Elaine found happiness with him.

One thought troubled Gittel after the marriage. Since Max was fourteen years older than Elaine, would her daughter be left a young widow? Gittel and Louis never lived long enough to find out.

Charles H. Freundlich

CONFRONTATIONS

SOL ATTENDED Yeshiva College for two years, was satisfied with the academic program, and especially with playing for the basketball team. He loved the camaraderie and traveling to other cities in New Jersey and Pennsylvania. He felt enriched by the courses in Modern Hebrew Literature which broadened his sense of Jewishness beyond the ancient Talmudic texts; and he felt greater pride in Israel and Zionism.

Sol admired Rabbi Dr. Brody, his Talmud teacher, who was unique in having a broad secular knowledge and a Ph.D.; and who presented his Talmud lectures in a modern critical manner. His lectures were delivered in English (unlike the other classes, which were presented in Yiddish).

Sol had originally been assigned to a rabbi who was a refugee, that escaped prior to the Holocaust. Like the other refugee rabbis that Yeshiva recently acquired, he was unfamiliar to America and modernity. He insisted on lecturing in Yiddish and looked with disdain at a college education.

"America, its language and culture was *goyish* [non-Jewish]. The pre-war world of Lithuanian culture had to be revived. The study of Torah, meaning the Babylonian Talmud, written in Aramaic, and its commentaries, was the only worthy endeavor. All other studies were *bitul Torah,* sinful, a waste of time," he declared

Sol viewed these refugee rabbis as misplaced, narrow fanatics, one-dimensional human beings, who were insulated from the modern world of science and culture. They were not congruent with the ideals of Yeshiva College students, who accepted modernity, and the desire to be part of the fabric of American life.

After a few months, Sol appealed to the Dean to transfer to Dr. Brody's class, asserting that he didn't understand Yiddish. It was ironic - the Dean did not speak English. Sol managed to convey his request in a broken Yiddish which convinced the Dean to make the transfer.

Sol esteemed Rabbi Brody for his knowledge of the philology and grammar of Semitic languages. A number of students from Boston and other out-of-town cities were also placed there because they did not know Yiddish. The class was known as the "Bum Class" because it was not conducted in Yiddish; though, the lectures were outstanding and scholarly.

Vyse Avenue

The following year, Sol entered the class of Rabbi Shusterman, a zealous proponent of *Talmud only* education. He was fractious and very hostile to modernity and English, and unable to fathom any viewpoint other than his own. His abrasive, extreme views offended even some of the more staid rabbis on the faculty.

Sol was dismayed with Rabbi Shusterman's hostility to America and its ideals of freedom of speech and religion. All Jewish ideologies, except his, were false and idolatrous. Sol considered him a bigot. After three months, Sol was miserable, having to listen for two hours to his ranting about *true Torah* versus compromised and *diluted Torah.*

Yeshiva College, Sol believed, was founded by rabbis who advocated a religious education combined with secular studies, without compromising Orthodox faith. This would enable Yeshiva graduates to take their place in modern society as productive citizens. This ideal was called *Torah Umadda*, Torah studies combined with science.

The new refugee rabbis thought this ideal was alien and profane. They survived the Holocaust by escaping from Poland and Lithuania, before the Nazi invasion in 1941, and gained shelter in Russia and Shanghai during the war. When they were brought to America, after the war, they tried to reproduce their Old World learning and lifestyle.

Unlike Sol's parents, who came to America as immigrants fleeing poverty and oppression, and eagerly seeking the American promise for a better life; the refugee rabbis had no desire to become part of the American dream. For them, America was *treif* [not kosher], a land where Jews assimilated and abandoned their faith. Only Eastern Europe was the natural home for Judaism. So, argued the *Chofetz*

Chaim (Israel Meir Kagan), the revered and universally acclaimed rabbinic luminary, in his book, *Nidchei Yisrael* (The Dispersed of Israel), in 1894. America, he argued, was a perilous land where Jews quickly forgot and desecrated their religious heritage. Those who had already emigrated should return to Europe - the secure environment for a religious life. Jewish immigrants should abandon the desire for economic gains in America and return to the spiritual safety in Poland and Lithuania. After the Holocaust, his disciples came as unwilling refugees, not to seek the American way of life.

Sol read about these rabbinic Cassandras who wished to thwart the huge wave of East European Jewish immigrants to America. They were less than successful among the poor and persecuted Jews who found safety and prosperity in the Land of Promise. A pity, Sol felt, that many remained in Europe and were killed in the Holocaust because of these imprudent rabbinic leaders.

Rabbi Shusterman was cynical towards Yeshiva College, though it provided him with a living. He insisted on conducting his class in Yiddish, asserting that English was unfit to teach Talmud. Once, he challenged Sol to translate a *Tosafos* [commentary], into English. Sol accepted the challenge, and translated the commentary into faultless English. Rabbi Shusterman was amused, but not convinced. In an acerbic rebuke to Sol's heresy, he exclaimed, "You will become a good American Rabbi." He could not imagine a more demeaning insult than calling a Jew, "American." On another occasion, he declared, "Yeshiva College needed a medical school because the yeshiva was sick!"

Vyse Avenue

SOL FELT that much of his Talmudic studies dealt with topics that seemed dysfunctional and irrelevant. He was bewildered by a number of themes:

How to deliver a *get,* [a writ of divorce] between Babylon and Israel,

How to acquire a bride through money, contract or sexual intercourse,

Marry a virgin on Wednesday,

Not to perform the first sexual intercourse with a virgin bride on the Sabbath,

Damages caused by oxen, whether through its horn, foot or tooth,

The four different methods of capital punishment, stoning, fire, sword, and strangulation,

Violating the Sabbath by carrying an object from home to street, which was a capital sin, punishable by stoning, if two witnesses gave warning,

How much ink (two letters) and how much paper (to write a divorce) must be carried to incur a violation of carrying on Sabbath and requiring a sacrifice or capital punishment,

Cursing God,

Adultery,

How many sacrifices to be brought to the Temple to atone for multiple, unintentional, Sabbath violations (hundreds of years after the Temple was destroyed)!

When Sol tried to explain his Talmud studies to his mother, she screamed, "Is this why I sent you to a yeshiva? A fourteen year old has to become an expert on sex, divorce and cutting off the head of a criminal? A *mishigas*, craziness - what are they filling your head with?"

171

There was little content in his Talmudic studies that Sol considered meaningful to his religious life. He wondered: Why not teach the parts of the Talmud that deal with the observances of daily life and holidays? Why not study the laws and customs to make Sabbath observance joyous and blissful - instead of the complex minutia describing the precise measure of items that were sinful if transferred from private to public domain? Why not study the numerous laws regarding ethics in family life and in society? Why not study the vast, non-legal, folklore called, *Aggadah* that included meaningful, fascinating and enlightening, moral tales of the rabbis? This, too, was the *Oral Torah*!

SOL'S MEETING with Professor Gutkind was most fortunate and illuminating. The Professor had moved to Vyse Avenue after accepting a post to head the Jewish Studies Department at a local college. He worshipped at the Heller Shtiebel and became the center of much gossip. Louis came home after Sabbath services and told Sol about the new member who was a famous scholar. Sol lost no time in introducing himself to the celebrity, as his neighbor. Professor Gutkind, middle-aged and slightly overweight, was affable and welcoming. Sol shared some of his reservations about the relevance of his Talmud studies.

Professor Gutkind had personally dealt with similar questions when he was a young yeshiva student in Poland, and was sympathetic to Sol's skepticisms. Though he no longer professed to be strictly Orthodox, he was traditional and respectful of the minutia of Orthodox rituals. He offered Sol a copy of an essay on Talmudic Scholarship, which he had prepared for a recent lecture. Perhaps, Sol would understand the nature of Talmudic thinking and logic, and appreciate the grandeur of the Talmudic world and how its purpose and content were often misunderstood throughout the ages. Sol kept a copy with him, and read it often, even when he went to Israel.

REFLECTIONS ON TALMUD STUDY
By H. Gutkind

THE TALMUD - the Oral Law delivered to Moses on Mt. Sinai - was first put to writing in a comprehensive code called the *Mishnah* about the year 200 C.E. Later scholars, called *Amoraim,* considered the very *text* of the Mishnah to be holy and cryptic like the Pentateuch, the Written Torah. Their commentary on the Mishnah, edited about the year 500 C.E. was called *Gemara* or *Talmud.*

The goal of traditional, Talmudic scholarship, in the various *yeshivot,* throughout the centuries, was to vindicate the profundity of each law and word of the text, and to resolve any apparent contradiction, with complex and often irrational theories and convoluted logic based on authoritative traditions. On the basis of the exegesis of the Talmud and its early commentaries, rabbis offered *teshuvot,* [rulings], to contemporary legal issues. For the medieval, pre-modern scholars, the Talmudic world was a complete universe, sequestered from the rest of the world.

At the later Breslau and Vienna Rabbinical Seminaries, the Talmud text was studied as a historic code of laws, subject to the influences of social and economic conditions of their society. Indeed, more than two-thousand words in the Talmud are of Greek or Roman origin. This

173

demonstrated that the Talmud was not a closed society but interacted with the greater Hellenic currents. The Talmud was a living document changing over the course of time. The rabbis of the Talmud did not claim to be prophets, nor were their opinions indisputable to their colleagues. They were great scholars and like other mortals, their opinions were fallible.

These modern critical approaches to the Talmud, (independent of earlier, medieval authorities) were deemed heretical in the Orthodox yeshivot. To the Orthodox mind, the ideal of Talmud study was the highest value of Judaism, a mitzvah comparable to all mitzvot. It served as an effective fortress of strength and survival for Jews and Judaism after the destruction of the Temple. The act of Talmud-Torah was the alpha and omega of Jewish creativity and intellectual endeavor. This passion for Talmud study would not change over the years.

What made Talmudic scholarship most challenging was the fact that the text was written in Aramaic, had no punctuation, or paragraphs. The laws of a particular topic were not presented in one place, but scattered throughout the Talmud. The Talmudic-Rabbinic editors may have presumed that a topical, orderly arrangement of the laws was not necessary for them. If a scholar devoted a lifetime to Talmud study, he didn't need these aids. Perhaps the editors did not realize that their confusing textual arrangement would morph into a second Written Torah, to be fixed, cryptic, and authoritative, and beyond the ken of the average layman.

To understand the depth of the problem, imagine the following:

A Telephone Directory in which the names are not listed alphabetically, or

Yellow Pages, that are not arranged according to topics, or,

A three thousand page law book, without a Table of Contents, or,

A road sign which points in opposite directions.

Indeed, the basic Talmudic text, known as the Mishnah, often cited two or three differing opinions. The *Amoraim*, the commentators, had to explain the meaning of the Mishnah, justify the logic of each opinion, and sometimes determine which opinion is authoritative - the final *halacha*, the practical law.

Sound confusing? Welcome to the Talmud.

No wonder that the study of Talmud was based on learning "how to learn!"

In the eleventh century, Rashi wrote a comprehensive commentary on the Talmud (as he did on the *Humash*) that was concise, authoritative and provided an excellent guide. His grandchildren, who expanded Rashi's commentary, sometimes differing with him, were known as the *Tosafos* (supplement). Rashi and his followers explained the content of the Talmud, but the problem was not the *content*, but the *confusing text*. The text, itself, had to be edited in a more orderly and logical fashion.

Was there no way to simplify the study of Talmudic law? Consider the revolutionary work of Moses Maimonides known in the yeshiva by his Hebrew initials, *RamBaM*.

In the twelfth century, the great rabbinic luminary and philosopher, Moses Maimonides, attempted to edit the *halacha* [the law], and fundamental principles in the chaotic, complex, corpus of the Talmud. In 1180, he wrote his *Mishneh Torah*, a Code of Law, for the layman, in clear and precise Hebrew, according to topics, including his decision of the final *halacha*. He eliminated the numerous, alternate legal opinions, eliminated the complicated exegesis, and made it simpler to find the law on a given topic. Gone were the abstruse debates of the *Gemara,* the comprehensive commentary of the Mishnah, which vindicated the texts but often were not relevant for practical application.

This prodigious work differed from earlier codes, which often included parts of the original Aramaic-Talmudic text. Maimonides was criticized by some scholars, and lionized by others, as the most authoritative rabbinic scholar.

In the course of years, Maimonides stature as *Posek* [authoritative judge], became universal. But his goal for simplicity, was weakened by his admirers who considered his *text*, holy, cryptic and worthy of exegesis. Thus, more commentaries were written about Maimonides' code, in the same spirit as the commentaries on the Talmud!

The study of Talmud, in Orthodoxy (not following Maimonides' paradigm), continued, all day and night, studying a commentary on a commentary on a commentary, ad infinitum - because all original *texts* were deemed holy and cryptic. Talmud study crowded out all other cultural endeavors for the yeshiva student. Music, art, science and literature were considered, *bitul Torah,* worthless, and sinful endeavors, because they detracted from Torah study.

The journey of many a devout yeshiva student, lacking secular and scientific knowledge - often led to his becoming a dysfunctional human being or a parasite. Only a few chosen of the Talmudic students became *Gedolim,*

[Great Ones], who became Deans in the cloistered yeshiva world.

Maimonides, who practiced medicine, was a prolific author. He wrote numerous tracts on logic, medicine, and philosophy in addition to his commentary (in Arabic) on the Mishnah, his monumental Code of Law, his *Guide for the Perplexed* (in Arabic) and his *Responsa* (in Judeo-Arabic). He should have served as a role model for future generations. One must engage in other sources of knowledge in addition to Talmud; Torah and secular wisdom can be in harmony.

However, later rabbis from Poland and Lithuania believed that there was no harmony, only conflict - no other studies than Talmud were permitted.

One Lithuanian Rabbi had more progressive views. As early as 1882, Rabbi Isaac Jacob Reines had advocated, in a Rabbinical Conference in St. Petersburg, Russia, the need to add secular studies and the Russian language to Talmud education. His views were denounced by his peers. But in 1905, he was successful in establishing such a school in Lida, Belorussia. In America, the Rabbi Isaac Elchanan Theological Seminary (part of Yeshiva University) which included a secular high school and college department was no doubt influenced by this liberal and modern view of Orthodox Judaism.

But other Lithuanian Rabbis, who came to America, established *yeshivot* in Brooklyn that did not allow secular studies, except those mandated by New York educational law. This did not include university education. They considered secular studies in college, heretical and dangerous.

Charles H. Freundlich

How did the noble ideal of Talmud-Torah become corrupted into the narrow and twisted program of text exegesis, devoid of practicality? It dates back to the incorrect understanding of the word "Torah" which means practical "instruction" for performing a mitzvah or holy act. Thus the Mishnah declared that Talmud-Torah was equal to all the other commandments because only through instruction could one know how to *perform a holy act.*

But after the Oral Torah, the Mishnah, was put to writing, it was erroneously thought that the *text* of the Mishnah, (not the content), was also Torah! Soon the *text* of the Gemara, the commentaries of the Mishnah, was given the status of *Torah from Mt. Sinai.* But the text of the Talmud was not written by Divine inspiration - but by fifth century Babylonian rabbis who spoke Aramaic!

Maimonides realized that the *halacha* (meaning observance), was being subordinated to textual analysis for its own sake (Torah *lishma*). The Mishnah declared, 'not the *Midrash* [textual analysis] is essential, but the *maaseh* [act].' There is a purpose for Torah study - to learn to act according to God's standards. *Textual analysis, devoid of practical observance, had to be replaced.* That was the great achievement of Maimonides' great code - restoring the *halacha*, the law, to the central purpose of Torah study. However, the paradigm he set was not usually pursued.

CONCLUSION: Instead of Talmud-Torah being a lucid pathway leading to religious observance, it diverged into an impractical, intellectual exercise, for its own sake - oblivious to life's numerous spiritual needs.

NEW HORIZONS

SOL WAS INSPIRED and enlightened, but conflicted, by Professor Gutkind's essay. How did this critical approach to Talmud - as a historical and legal code written by scholars and influenced by social and economic factors - harmonize with Orthodox tradition - that the Talmud was The Oral Torah, received by Moses on Mt. Sinai? He was comforted to know that a great scholar like Maimonides, (who was Orthodox in his belief in the sanctity and authority of the Talmud), appreciated the problems of the *text* for the ordinary layman, and tried to correct it.

Sol believed that Yeshiva should have appointed rabbis, in the spirit of Maimonides, who were supportive of Torah education combined with modern secular knowledge.

Charles H. Freundlich

Sol was not alone. Many of the Yeshiva students were facing the same predicament. But if everyone was studying the Talmud text as the word of God, from Mt. Sinai, then it must be truthful and relevant. This Talmudic world, sequestered from modern life, Sol felt, was pathological, a collective delusion. But within this cloistered world, the Sea of the Talmud was joyous, fulfilling and spiritually uplifting. Reality gave way to emotional faith.

Following Professor Gutkind's advice, Sol read the multi-volume, *History of the Jews*, by Heinrich Graetz, and it was an epiphany. He realized that the Talmud had a history and development, and could be studied as a human document written by human beings, not infallible, heavenly spirits.

He learned that rabbinic scholars like Nachman Krochmal, Zechariah Frankel, and I.H. Weiss, in the nineteenth century, approached the laws and text of the Talmud as a human, historic document, developing and changing in the course of centuries, as a response to changes in society. The customs and laws cited in the Talmud, they believed, may have been ancient and some originated on Mt. Sinai, but the *text* was neither divine nor cryptic. They used critical tools like philology, comparative law and religion, ancient manuscripts, and historical records, to explain the *text*, without the *pilpul,* the hair-splitting exegesis, which defied credulity.

Sol, and other Yeshiva students, would have to adapt, and compromise their modernity with the accepted, traditional Talmudic scholarship. Take it or leave it. For Sol, and others, the transfer to a more liberal Seminary - Conservative, or Reform, (where modern scholarship was pervasive), was reprehensible.

Vyse Avenue

Traditional yeshiva students lacking a modern education often became narrow, unskilled, human beings - *melamdim,* petty religious functionaries, or parasites. Only a few chosen of the Talmudic students became *Gedolim* [Great Ones], who became luminaries in the cloistered yeshiva world.

Some students abandoned Yeshiva College because of the antiquated views of Rabbi Shusterman and similar rabbis. Many of the most talented graduates transferred to the Jewish Theological Seminary, a Conservative rival, for ordination. This caused distress in the Yeshiva administration and a restructuring of its own Ordination Program

Sol was among those who left at the end of the semester, after much soul-searching. Among those who preceded him were Yeshiva College graduates who became renowned Conservative Rabbis: Joseph Yerushalmi, the eminent Jewish historian at Harvard and Columbia - Aaron Landes (President of the Student Organization of Yeshiva), became a prominent rabbi in Philadelphia, and a Rear Admiral, the highest ranking Chaplain in the U.S.Naval Reserve - and Chaim Potok, an esteemed man of letters, an editor of The Jewish Publication Society, a historian, and an acclaimed novelist. Potok also portrayed, in a best-selling novel, the stormy, religious disputes between the refugee rabbis and the moderate rabbis at Yeshiva. Other novels of Potok dealt with the tension between Orthodox Judaism, modernity, and the quest for artistic freedom.

Sol was engrossed by a confrontation which took place in the halls of Yeshiva regarding the annual Dean's Night. Students brought their girlfriends to attend this annual entertaining program presented by the students. These programs, according to some, crossed the lines of Orthodox propriety. Rabbi Shusterman protested vigorously. It was heresy to allow women to mix freely at a Yeshiva program, and he forbade his students from attending. However, another eminent rabbi defended the program calling Rabbi Shusterman's uproar, "sanctimonious." Rabbi Shusterman lashed out, "I no longer consider you a *tzaddik*!" The acrimonious controversy eventually forced the annual event to be held in a more modest venue - the basement. Some believed that this incident presaged the beginning of Yeshiva's shift to the right.

Sol decided to transfer to Brooklyn College. This was a radical life-altering experience. He would be leaving the sheltered, spiritual world of yeshiva learning and the exuberant joy of the basketball team. His two-year career at Yeshiva's basketball squad was undistinguished. A sole outstanding scoring performance against Lycoming College in Williamsport, PA, was reported in the local press. He pondered, am I ready for this extreme change?

Sol attended Brooklyn College during the daytime and majored in pre-med. He found the program easy, compared to the long hours at Yeshiva College, with its double program of religious and secular studies. What would he do with this additional time? He found a part-time job in a bakery and was delighted to bring home some money, in addition to the free cakes, which were eagerly devoured by his brothers. Once again, he and his brothers enjoyed the Boston Crème and Seven-layer cakes reminiscent of the time when their parents operated a bakery shop on Jennings Street.

Vyse Avenue

He began to read serious literature during his one-hour subway ride to Brooklyn. By the end of the first month, Sol had read more than thirty books on philosophy, politics and classical literature. He also read some of the Jewish classics, including the *Kuzari* by Yehuda Halevi and the *Guide for the Perplexed* by Maimonides, in English translations. These works broadened his horizons; and he began appreciating the depth and beauty of Judaism beyond the dry, legalistic, Talmud studies. The more he read, the greater was his thirst for literature. He decided to switch his major to English Literature.

Intensive reading transformed Sol's life and perspective, especially towards Jewish tradition. He viewed the secular student life at Brooklyn College as frivolous, empty, and unfulfilling. Most of the students were focused on a life of fun, sexual gratification and career. There was no spirit of learning or achieving excellence of character. Their language was vulgar, filled with sexual allusions. What good is freedom, he reflected, when it was lacking a discipline of ideals and worthy goals?

Sol felt disenchanted with the Jewish students at Brooklyn College, who were highly assimilated, lacking in Jewish knowledge and values. The six-month experience in the non-yeshiva world was a profound disappointment and failure. Sol felt desolate. Where could he turn next? The personal fulfillment he sought would have to be found in returning to the yeshiva world.

In September, Sol registered to attend a Brooklyn yeshiva that allowed its students to attend college in the evening. Sol was now studying Talmud from nine to five and traveling to Brooklyn College for evening sessions. His daily rides on the subway afforded him more time for serious reading.

The Brooklyn *Mesivta* had a variety of Talmud teachers, some acculturated to America, and a few refugees. During his first year, his teacher was a traditional scholar and approached the text in a cryptic way, finding deeper meaning in every word. He did not know Aramaic grammar and less about modern critical methods, but Sol appreciated his sincere approach to the text as the literal word of God, orally communicated to Moses on Mt. Sinai.

In his second year, his teacher was a scion of famous Lithuanian scholars whose method involved a critical analysis of the text. His father had been an esteemed Talmud teacher in Poland before coming to the United States. This teacher was young and modern, and his relationship to the students was affable. He often discussed current issues of Jewish life at the end of the formal lectures.

Some of the more sectarian rabbis of the yeshiva were displeased with this rabbi's liberal views: He did not consider shaving during the *sefirah* period sinful, since the prohibitions of *sefirah-mourning* were not rooted in Talmudic sources. More controversial, was his ruling, after being questioned by his students, that it was not necessary to wear a skullcap while attending college classes. He deemed wearing a skullcap, "a nice, pious custom, not a required law." Sol followed his advice. Others followed the opinion of another rabbi in the *Mesivta*, who ruled that walking bareheaded was an egregious Torah violation - an imitation of the idolatrous non-Jews (even in college).

Sol began writing articles for the Brooklyn-based *Jewish Press* along with some of his fellow students. He began by contributing book- reviews; and then, added serious political and social commentary. As his reading progressed, Sol became more committed to Israel and Zionism; and his columns became a very powerful advocacy of Israeli politics, to the dismay of the more traditional elements of the Mesivta.

He contacted his old Vyse Avenue neighbor and mentor, Jackie, now an executive of the Zionist Mizrachi Youth, and was hired to be a leader at one of their branches. Many of the students at the Mesivta were active members of the B'nei Akiva, a religious Zionist organization that encouraged *aliyah*. Sol soon envisioned a trip to the seven– year old State of Israel. How could he achieve this?

A notice in the Mizrachi Bulletin announced that they were sponsoring scholarships for a year-long study program in a yeshiva in Rehovot that was supported by the Rabbinical Council of America. Sol was interviewed and informed that he had the requisite qualifications in Talmud and Zionism. He would be responsible to pay for the cost of the ship tickets. The committee would review his application and inform him shortly. He knew he could earn enough money by working in the Catskills in the summer. With bated breath, Sol awaited the decision.

Two weeks after his interview, Sol received the letter of acceptance and was ecstatic. "Mamma, I was accepted. I was accepted! Please come." Gittel hurried from the kitchen holding a large spoon with which she was stirring soup; and she beheld her son, in the living room, jumping with joy. "What's burning? Where's the fire? Accepted to what?" Gittel asked.

"I was accepted to a study program in Israel sponsored by the Zionist organization with a full scholarship." Gittel found it surprising. "Why do you have to go to Israel? Isn't your yeshiva in America good enough?"

Sol was nonplussed. "Of course my yeshiva is good enough. But this is America, the land of promise - not the Promised Land. Israel is our Jewish homeland! Israel is the land for which we prayed for two thousand years. Seven years ago, the State of Israel was reborn. What could be more wonderful than studying in Israel for a year?"

Gittel sat down gingerly and was not convinced. "I understand your joy, Sol; but Israel is thousands of miles away. Daddy and I won't be there for you - we will miss you."

"I'll miss you too, Mamma. But this is a chance of a lifetime, studying in Israel."

"I'm worried. What about the *Fedayeen* sneaking into Israel and killing Jews?"

"Don't worry, Mamma. I'll be safe in a group with other Americans from other yeshivas. The Arabs wouldn't dare kill American students; Eisenhower won't let them. America is still the greatest and most powerful nation on earth."

"So, if America is the greatest country, why are you running off to Israel like a poor immigrant?"

Sol was exasperated and showed the letter to his mother. "See, it indicates that after my interview last month, I was selected to receive a year's scholarship to a yeshiva in Rehovot, not far from Tel Aviv. Food and dorm are covered; I only have to pay for the ship tickets both ways."

Gittel could not identify with Sol's jubilation. She felt that her gifted son, with outstanding academic achievement in school, was leaving home, and would be gone for a year.

She recollected how she was desolate when her father bade her to immigrate to America, to earn some money for her dowry, and send some home. She mused about the thrill of coming to America, seeing the Statue of Liberty, and passing the special examinations in Ellis Island. This was the greatest country. What's wrong with these youth, running all over the world to find Paradise? Don't they know that Paradise is here in New York, the greatest Jewish city in the world? We have everything here - only four blocks from Jennings Street - no pogroms, and no passing armies. It was safe in America for Jews. "Let me see what Leibel has to say."

When Louis heard the news, he was filled with excitement. He cried, "The land of Israel, *Eretz Yisrael*, the Holy Land! We are proud of you, Sol. Study hard and be successful. Wait till I tell Rabbi Heller that my son was chosen to study in Israel with a full scholarship."

When Louis kissed Sol, his face radiated joy; and there were tears in his eyes. Louis began dancing through the house, jumping wildly, as was the custom of his Hassidic father. He understood the significance of Sol's opportunity, having prayed three times daily, for the rebuilding of Jerusalem and the ushering in of the Messianic Era. The long, bitter, exile would be over; universal peace and joy would reign. His son Sol, the son of Louis Friedman, was now part of this greatest moment in Jewish history.

"Let's sit down and discuss this," Gittel said nervously. "First, how are we going to pay for the ship tickets to Israel?"

Sol countered, "I'll work at the Evergreen this summer. Remember how well I did at the Evergreen four years ago? I can earn more than nine hundred dollars in the dining room, enough to cover the cost of the tickets."

"Number two, what will you accomplish there on the other side of the world that you can't accomplish here, in America? Will you become a rabbi?"

Sol argued, "I think so. I know that a number of American students study for the s*emicha,* ordination, test in Israel, and are granted certificates by the Chief Rabbinate. I'll take along my volume of *Yoreh Deah*, which deals with the Kashrut laws for the *semicha* test. I can do it in one year."

Gittel cautioned, "Sol, you are twenty-one and are finishing college. You will have to work and get a job. So don't come home without s*emicha.* You'll make the whole family proud if you are ordained as a rabbi; you'll make a living. One more thing, what about your attendance at the *Mesivta*? Are you leaving for good or will you continue when you return?"

"I'll take a leave of absence and probably continue for a year or so."

The family meeting was over, and Sol's brothers, who were in the army serving in Korea, would be informed, by mail, about the exciting family news. Gittel phoned her daughter, Elaine, in Jersey. "Wonderful news - Sol won a scholarship to study in Israel and we are all so proud."

"Israel? That's so far away, and it's dangerous," Elaine responded.

"Nonsense," replied Gittel. "The Arabs wouldn't dare harm American students - Eisenhower won't let them! America is still the most powerful country."

The following day, Sol made an appointment to meet with the *Rosh Ha-yeshiva*, the Dean of the *Mesivta*. What would he say? He had never spoken to the Dean on a personal level, and there was the issue of his scholarship to the Mesivta, based on need. Most students received a full or partial scholarship and only a select group of wealthy students paid the full tuition. How would he justify his expensive trip to Israel?

He entered the outer office of the Dean and after the buzzer sounded, walked gingerly into the inner office. He remained standing for a few moments, until the Dean signaled that he may sit.

The Dean was corpulent, with a full grey beard that covered his cheeks and reached almost to his dark eyes, which peered out from a black-framed pair of glasses. His eyes sparkled. He was wearing a black caftan, a white shirt buttoned to the top and a gray tie. He was silent for a moment, and then closed a large thick volume on his glass covered desk. He looked at Sol as if examining his soul, wondering - who is this young man?

"Your name is Friedman, Sol Friedman from the Bronx? You must travel more than an hour each way. Very commendable, and you receive the reward of the mitzvah of traveling in addition to the mitzvah of learning Torah."

"Yes. I'm one of the few who commutes daily from the Bronx. The advantage is that each hour on the train permits me to do a lot of reading."

"What do you read?"

"I love books on Jewish philosophy, Yehuda Halevi, Maimonides and Saadia Gaon."

"Very profound books - for a young man."

"I also read secular classics, the writings of Plato, Spinoza and Nietzsche."

189

"I'm surprised. They are dangerous books, contrary to the Torah. You should avoid them."

"I believe that an Orthodox Jew must also be acquainted with the great thinkers of the modern world, in addition to the Talmud."

"Secular books should be permitted only to a *talmid chacham*, an advanced scholar, whose faith in Torah is secure and deeply rooted. I fear that these secular books can uproot genuine faith for a young man, such as you. You may check with me, before reading such dangerous, non-Torah books. Tell me, what else do you do?"

"I've been writing articles for the *Jewish Press*, mostly book- reviews."

"Yes, I recall that you wrote some interesting articles for the Jewish Press. But, I did not approve of what you wrote recently about Orthodox girls required to do National Service in Israel. I understand your viewpoint about Zionism. We have many *talmidim* [students],who belong to Zionist groups, but they are more circumspect. They consult me *before* expressing controversial views. I have asked one of our outstanding *talmidim,* to meet with you in order to bring your views in harmony with the authentic, uncompromised, Torah viewpoint."

"I thank the Dean for taking such a personal interest in me and my writings, and I look forward to further guidance."

"I am pleased. Now, why have you come? What can I do for you?"

"I ask permission of the Dean to take a leave of absence for a year so that I can pursue further studies in a yeshiva in Israel. I have already received notice of my acceptance to one in Rehovot."

"You have made plans to study in Israel *prior to my permission*? That is not respectful."

"I ask the Dean's pardon. I was so excited about the program I thought there would be no objection."

"Is this a Zionist yeshiva or an Orthodox yeshiva?"

"I believe it is Orthodox because it is sponsored by the *Orthodox Rabbinical Council of America* and by the *Mizrachi*."

"I do not understand this contradiction - either Orthodox or Zionist. However I have no objections to your studying Torah in the Holy Land. How does your father feel about your leaving America? I do not know much about your family. What does your father do for a living?"

"My father works in a factory in Long Island. He is a loving and kind father."

"You say, *loving*. Is he learned? Is he a Sabbath observer?"

"My father is very hard- working, and is devoted to his family. He is not a scholar."

"Is he observant?"

"He went to *heder* in the Old Country and learned his Judaism from his Hassidic father. He *davens* every day puts on *tefillin* and makes the *motzi* before every meal. He observes the Sabbath as best he can."

"An unlearned father, who is not a Sabbath observer, how can you live in the same house with such a man?"

Sol was offended, and his heart was beating faster. "He is my father. He loves me and I love him."

"But he is unlearned, and an unlearned person cannot be religious! He will influence you and undermine your study of Torah! Maybe it's best that you leave your home for a year and study in Israel. You have my permission for a leave of absence for a year and I extend my blessings to you. Go in peace, return in peace, and may you be successful in your Torah studies and a credit to the Mesivta. You may leave now."

Sol lowered his head and walked backwards out of the office. The Dean was patently displeased with Sol for a number of reasons, and the feelings were reciprocal. Sol mused, how is it possible not to be thrilled with the idea of studying in Israel? Does he think that Brooklyn is the Holy Land?

When Sol left the Dean's office, stepping backwards, a sign of respect that was de rigueur, he was exasperated. He felt his soul was crushed; that he had committed a sin in loving his father; committed a crime for being a Zionist, and having accepted the opportunity of studying in Israel. He felt belittled. Is this what one expects after an encounter with a world-renowned Talmudic scholar? He showed no humanity or compassion! This confrontation with the Dean reverberated in Sol's mind for years.

Sol phoned the maître d'hotel at the Evergreen Country Club. He remembered Sol, and immediately hired him to work in the dining room.

Sol had two months to prepare for his Israel trip. Gittel wrote to her cousins in Rishon L'Zion, Ra'anana, and Tel Aviv, to welcome him, and to look after his needs. Since 1947, Gittel had been sending packages of clothes to her cousins who wrote about their financial straits in Palestine and when Israel became a state.

Sol consulted a few fellow students who had returned from Israel on educational programs. They briefed him about the many items that were expensive and in short supply: camera film, nylon shirts, electric shavers, toilet paper, and cosmetics. He would have to bring gifts for his relatives, survivors of the Holocaust, who were the remnants of the large families of his parents in Austria-Hungary and Poland.

SUMMER ARRIVED, and Sol was happy to be back at The Evergreen Country Club, where he enjoyed many happy experiences. The work in the dining room was often tedious and stressful as a busboy. But the anticipation of going to Israel was a great source of comfort. There were some cosmetic changes in the Evergreen in the four years since his first job there. Basketball was eliminated after the 1951 scandals at City College, L.I.U. and other colleges. A fully air-conditioned, luxury building, was available for affluent clients. Pincus, the captain of the waiters, was still there, as was, the maître d', Mr. Weiner. But the members of the athletic staff, whom he idolized, did not return.

Sol worked hard, but had time to read, swim, play basketball and enjoy the sunny afternoons before dinner. He loved to walk along the dirt road from the hotel to the village amid stately Pine and Oak trees, dressed casually in shorts and tee shirt. He also enjoyed the shows in the Playhouse, especially on Saturday nights.

One incident marred his idyllic summer. Two counselors from the day camp drove to New York early in the morning on their day off. After lunch, that day, the tragic news reached the hotel. Both counselors were killed when their car ran off the road. It was a shocking episode for the staff and the funerals in New York were attended by hundreds.

This tragic occurrence shook Sol's faith in the benevolence of God's world. The rustic Paradise he had found in the Catskills was flawed. Would his study in Israel provide a deeper understanding of life and its tragedies?

HOMECOMING

THE VOYAGE on the *Jerusalem*, an old refurbished ship, provided Sol with an orientation to Israel. The daily announcements in Hebrew and English and the conversations with the swarthy Israeli crew, were a delight to his ears. Among the many passengers were students, including the fifteen in his program, who were filled with passionate Zionist ideals. Sol began to read a Hebrew novel by Agnon, and had serious discussions about the possibility of permanent a*liyah.*

One member of his group was from Mexico, and the rest were from New York. The crossing of the Atlantic was turbulent and Sol was sea-sick for two days. The ship made one stop in Naples, and then crossed through the Mediterranean into clement waters for three more days.

As they approached the shores of Haifa, Sol felt ecstatic at the sight of the buildings nestled on the mountainside. Was this what the immigrants experienced when they saw the Statue of Liberty? Adela, his cousin, her husband Emil, and their son, Sammy, were waiting for hours on shore, in a jeep. They embraced him with great emotion like a long-lost relative and Sol felt bonded to them.

As they drove south to Tel Aviv, Sol recalled the information Gittel had given him about this branch of the family and their survival from the Holocaust. Louis' older brother, Shmuel, had remained in Polish Lvov, formerly Lemberg, after World War I. He prospered, but was later shot by the Polish police on suspicion of being a German spy because he did not speak Polish. Shmuel spoke only German, the language of Lemberg, before Galicia became annexed to the greater Poland. Shmuel's daughter, Adela, remained in Lvov, married and survived with her second husband, Emil, a successful and renowned photographer.

Adela had two daughters, Yula and Irene (with her first husband), and Sammy with Emil. In 1939, after the German invasion of Poland, they all fled east through Russia to central Asia and finally arrived in Palestine. They established their home and business in Tel Aviv. Adela was about the same age as Louis, and was Sol's first cousin. Adela's two daughters, Yula and Irene, were married in Palestine and they and their husbands fought in Israel's War of Independence in 1948. Yula's son, Michael, was four years old, and Irene's daughter, Beruriah, was eight. Sammy,

Adela's son from her second marriage, was the same age as Sol and he became a dear and close friend.

Sol realized that he was more than a cousin. He was an *American,* a symbol of inspiration and hope for all immigrants - even those who settled in Israel. He was the *American cousin*, not quite rich, but prosperous. Sol came to Israel to deepen his Jewish identity; but for the first time in his life, he felt more like an American - not a child of immigrants; and he began to wear this American identity with pride.

During his first three months, Sol studied at the Rehovot yeshiva and visited his relatives in Tel Aviv on the week-end. They were not religiously observant, but they did try to accommodate Sol with Kosher food and Sabbath observance. Both Yula and Irene would compete to have Sol as their guest. On occasion, Sol would baby-sit for Yula's son, Michael, when they went out on a Saturday evening.

Sol adjusted to the Spartan diet at the yeshiva, and looked forward to the many *tiyulim* (tours), throughout Israel, arranged by the administration. The classes were conducted in Hebrew and this enhanced Sol's language skill. But surrounded with the American students in the program, he tended to speak in English. The teachers were young, excellent, inspiring, and very Zionistic. Sol advanced his knowledge of Talmud and the land of Israel

The one draw-back was the age of the Israeli students, mostly teenagers in high school. Some of the Americans left for Jerusalem, to attend the historic Hevron or Mir yeshivas, hoping to receive ordination. At the end of December, Sol left to attend the renowned, *Yeshivat Mercaz HaRav*, in Jerusalem, with its modern orientation and Zionist ideology. Most of the students were high school graduates, were attending university, or were army veterans. Unlike the other yeshivas in Jerusalem, the classes were conducted in Hebrew and included lectures on modern themes. As the only American student, Sol advanced his Hebrew knowledge by total immersion.

Sol began to prepare seriously for his *semicha* (ordination) exam, and spent hours mastering the *Yoreh Deah,* part of the code of Jewish law which was a basic requisite. In addition to being qualified, he had to present documentation, letters of approval from the Deans of Israeli yeshivas, where he attended.

After almost a year's study, the Deans of the yeshivas in Rehovot and in Jerusalem provided official letters replete with encomiums of his character and scholarship. Sol made an appointment with the office of the Chief Rabbinate to begin the formal tests.

The first step was an examination by the local religious court, the *Beth Din*, on the laws of the *Yoreh Deah.* Sol passed the test with ease. The final step was a personal interview and comprehensive test in Talmud by the Chief Rabbi, Isaac Halevy Herzog.

9:00 A.M.   SOL SAT nervously by the desk of the Chief Rabbi of Israel. He was conscious that this test was the summation of more than ten years of intensive study of Torah. His dream of being a rabbi would be realized or shattered in one day. It felt like Yom Kippur in the presence of the Divine Court where his soul was being judged and every act carefully weighed.

Vyse Avenue

HE HAD HEARD numerous stories about the Chief Rabbi and his international reputation, his broad secular education, in law and literature, in addition to Talmud. He was distinguished from most of the rabbis who were schooled exclusively in Talmud and had not graduated from university.

Born in Lomza, Poland, the Chief Rabbi came to Leeds, England, as a youth with his father, who would serve as the rabbi. After attending the Sorbonne and the University of London, he received his Ph.D., having written a remarkable doctoral dissertation; he had discovered the long-lost source of the blue dye for the ritual fringes of the *tallit.*

He went on to serve as the Rabbi in Belfast and Dublin, becoming Ireland's Chief Rabbi for more than a decade. After the demise of Abraham Isaac Kook, the First Chief Rabbi of Palestine (as the British mandate was called), he became the Chief Rabbi. His background was impressive and Sol felt anxiety.

Sol recalled the practical briefing from his friends: "Don't take the test on a Friday morning and don't speak English." The problem was - on Friday mornings, rabbis from all over Israel, would come to the Chief Rabbi's office to court his favor. The second note of caution was the Chief Rabbi's English. The elderly Chief Rabbi, who had a flowing white beard and was dressed in a black caftan, spoke with a distinct Irish brogue - a peculiarity that often evoked a subtle smile or a sense of amazement from American tourists.

9:15 A.M. THE CHIEF RABBI entered the room wearing a house-robe and slippers. Sol stood up. He was surprised to see him dressed so casually. The Rabbi asked in

199

Hebrew, "In which language shall we conduct the test?" Sol knew that Yiddish was the mother tongue of the Chief Rabbi and was a slight handicap for him. English was out. He replied, "Hebrew." The Rabbi quickly scanned the letters of recommendation which Sol had received from the two Deans, Rabbi Zvi Yehuda Meltzer and Rabbi Zvi Yehuda Kook. He looked up at Sol with a smile, having read their exaggerated encomiums as if to surmise, "We shall see."

When the Chief Rabbi reached for the first volume of the Talmud, his secretary dashed into the office, "Your Excellency, there is an emergency." He then whispered a few words. The Chief Rabbi turned to Sol, "We shall have to continue the exam tomorrow at 9:00 a.m."

Sol had been warned about these interruptions by the local rabbinate. If it were not an issue of public Sabbath violations in Jerusalem, or the legitimacy of a conversion document, there were scores of problems to which regional rabbis turned to the Chief Rabbi. In particular, he had close diplomatic relations with the Pope over the reclaiming of young Jewish children and orphans rescued by monasteries, or hidden by Gentile families during the Holocaust - many of whom were baptized. The complexity of reclaiming Jewish children whom the Church deemed saved by baptism, was most painful for all - even to the orphans who had been practicing Catholicism.

It was Wednesday, and Sol felt safe from the threat of the Friday morning assemblies. He had one more day to review some basic Talmud texts, and to think about his preparations for this final exam. He returned to his room and tried to rest. But his mind was filled with many thoughts and preparations for the test. Sol had indicated that he had studied sections of ten different *Mesechtos* (volumes), of Talmud.

The test weighed heavily upon his soul. His mother had charged him before he left, "Don't come home without semicha. You are twenty-one and will have to work." He would officially be a *rabbi*, a title that was held in great veneration and pride by his family. Coming home without *semicha,* would be humiliating - a disappointment to his family.

Sol walked along the crowded Jaffa Street hoping to put aside the burden of the test, but he could not. He recalled the long hours of work as a waiter in the crowded dining room of the Evergreen, the previous summer, and the *nudniks* who bothered him with requests for warm milk, extra butter, freshly squeezed orange juice, and the double portions of cooked prunes. He recalled with laughter, the fact that the largest and most lavish meal was the luncheon on *Tisha B'Av*, one of the fast days on the Jewish calendar.

Sol had written to his parents almost every day, and they responded at least once a week. He treasured each letter from home, and read them often sensing the closeness of their feelings of love and concern for him. The handwriting from his father was artistic and his mother's was distinctive.

October 15, 1955

Dear Sol,

I am so happy to hear from you and remember, I love you very much. About the package for your cousins in Tel Aviv, don't worry if they send it back I wouldn't be angry. I was today downtown and bought myself two nice dresses, a housecoat and a pair of shoes. Did you see my Tante Leah or

Sophie? Nothing new, around here. Jackie called and so did the rabbi. Did you deliver all the gifts that your friends told you to bring? Do you need any money? You can borrow from Henry and we will pay back the money to his parents. You say you are losing weight. Are you sick? Please, take care of yourself. We love you. We sent a package to the Shekels with dresses, white shirts, the size he asked for, and ties. It is a gift from us. But for the Mix Master which they asked for, it will cost about thirty dollars. They will pay you in Israeli money. Last week we went to HIAS to find out about sending an affidavit for Sammy to come to America. Unfortunately, we do not earn enough, they told us. Did you get the package from Elaine? She sent coffee and other food. If you buy gifts for us, I would like a silver Sabbath candlestick; Daddy would like a holiday machzor without the English. For Elaine and Max, you can buy a Siddur with the English. Tomorrow I am going to visit Todros and remember I love you.

Ma

P.S. If you want and if you have time visit the brother of the grocer on Jennings St... You have time when you are on vacation. I think he is a teacher. He is expecting you any time and lives on Rechov Derech Haifa 23. That is all for today. *F.G.*

"F.G." meant *Fat Gittel* and reflected her acceptance of her obesity as part of her identity. Much of the correspondence dealt with sending gifts to his relatives or sending additional money, and repeating: He was not to get involved if there were war with Egypt; why was he losing weight, didn't they feed him in the yeshiva? The one item that caused some friction was Sol's previous request to send Adela a Mix Master, for which she would reimburse Sol in Israeli money. However, this required some technical red-tape in addition to the 220 electrical current, and was beyond the grasp of Gittel. Eventually, after numerous letters citing the aggravation, and two months of shopping, the Mix Master arrived and Adela was elated.

Sol went to the nearby Falafel shop for a light lunch and then returned to his room to rest. He began to think about his relatives in Israel who had become his new family. He penned this letter to his parents:

Dear Mamma and Daddy,

Only a few weeks more before I return home on the S.S.Zion, on June 1. What a year this has been! From the first day that I stepped off the boat in Haifa our Israeli relatives treated me with love - the kind of love I receive from you. I spent the last week-end with Irene who is called, "Irka," and her family in Tel Aviv. Though they are not religious, they purchased special Kosher barbecued chicken for Shabbat. During the week, I eat breakfast at her home, usually a salad and a hard-boiled egg and the instant coffee I brought from America. I consider Irka my sister and I respect her husband, Erik, who is very gracious and punctilious. The coffee was really appreciated by everyone - it's so expensive here.

I go out for lunch. There's a very reasonable meat restaurant on Dizengoff St. We had some cake baked by Adela who was so thankful for the Mix Master you sent. She is blind in one eye and really appreciated this machine because she does a lot of baking. They paid me for it in Israeli money. They don't like to receive gifts. They are comfortable, but they are grateful for the special electronic, kitchen appliances that are so expensive here and cost less in America.

Let me assure you that I am well and have enough money to cover my expenses. Remember the ten nylon shirts that I brought with me? A cabby admired them and I sold him eight shirts. He felt he got a terrific bargain, though I bought them for less. We both did well from the sale.

Last week, I went shopping for souvenirs: for Daddy - a silver cigarette holder, a tie clip with colored stones, and leather bound holiday siddur - for Mamma, a decorated challah cover and a silver candle-stick. I also bought a number of trinkets: a candy dish, ash tray, fruit bowl and a number of blue patina ash-trays for the house. They were not expensive but they were typical of Israeli art. I also bought a number of books that my friend, Bernie, will take with him when he returns to America. Marvin, another class mate, will take home some of the gifts I bought for you. They are returning to America before me and they will call you when they arrive.

How are things with Seymour and Marvin in Korea? Do you get mail often? Is Elaine expecting another child? I hope it's a girl.

I love you all and look forward to coming home, even though I consider Israel my home.

Sol

P. S. I'm in the midst of taking some important tests this week. I'll let you know how I made out. Please send my regards to my friends and class mates who ask about me.

Vyse Avenue

SOL ASSURED his parents that this trip was his financial responsibility, and he did not want them to send money. They felt both pride and honor that their son was a recipient of a scholarship to study in the Holy Land. They still called it *Palestine* or the *Holy Land,* rather than *Eretz Yisrael.*

They worried about the threat of war with Egypt. Israel had been created seven years earlier, fought valiantly and successfully for its independence, yet, was experiencing the tragic episodes of *Fedayeen*, terrorists, crossing the borders, and casting a pall of fear throughout the land. His mother cautioned, "If there is a war, don't get involved. You're an American, not an Israeli." But he felt indignant, and wrote her, "Mamma, we are all Jews in America and in Israel." With the threat of war with Egypt, he knew that he would have to weigh the depths of his dual identity as a Jew and as an American.

He thought about his fellow students in the program and their diverse backgrounds. Some of the students were upper middle-class, and they received a letter from their rabbi who declared that in case of war, they were not required to volunteer. However, their rabbi in *Yeshivat HaDarom* told them that in case of war, it was a sacred mitzvah for all, including Americans, to join in the defense of Israel.

HOW QUICKLY THE YEAR HAD PASSED. He recalled the first few months upon arrival in Israel after a weary trip aboard the "Jerusalem." Sea-sickness had taken more than eight pounds off his slender body. He marveled at the muscular and swarthy crew. "*Hakshivu tsevet, hakshivu kol hanosim*, attention crew, attention all passengers," reverberated in his mind and it was a glorious moment to observe Jewish sailors and waiters speaking Hebrew.

He noticed that life on board included sexual encounters which the crew had arranged for the passengers. One evening, he was scheduled to tutor, Sheldon, a fellow student, who was deficient in Talmud. Fearing a placement test, Sheldon asked Sol for some assistance. They were to meet in the ship's small Chapel. But when the scheduled time arrived, Sol was greeted by a member of the crew, "Sheldon sent me to tell you that he cannot meet with you. I've arranged for him to meet a very lovely girl."

Sol felt disgust. How could a rabbinical student on his way to the Israel, rebuff his studies for a date, perhaps a prostitute? The following day, he overheard a conversation between Sheldon and Dr. Kramer, a prominent Hebrew Scholar.

"I plan to attend the *Seminary* next year, following my study in Israel," Sheldon reported.

"Excellent. You have made a wise decision leaving the yeshiva world. Your future as a rabbi will be more secure as a Conservative Rabbi," Dr. Kramer replied, as he patted Sheldon on the cheek. Sol thought to himself, "Good riddance!"

HE RECALLED THAT CONSUMMATE MOMENT – his arrival at Haifa and meeting his relatives from Tel Aviv who were waiting with great anticipation on shore. Adela, the matriarch of the family, spoke mostly German, but greeted Sol in Yiddish. The other relatives spoke to Sol in Hebrew. His relatives had been in contact with his own parents, through the efforts of HIAS, and a lengthy correspondence ensued including sending packages to them.

Adela's son, Sammy, owned a scooter and they would ride together down Allenby, the busiest street in Tel Aviv. Sammy assisted his father, Emil, in the photography shop, and he was an expert in this field. Though Sammy was born in Poland, he had come as a youth to Palestine and was like a native *Sabra*. He spoke Polish with his mother and sisters, but in Hebrew to Sol, and they were close as brothers.

A VIVID MEMORY that challenged his idealistic view of Israel took place on the third day of his arrival in Rehovot. It was Friday evening, and one of the Israeli students was bitten by a scorpion and needed medical attention. The Dean of the yeshiva allowed the telephone call to the hospital to be made, overriding the Sabbath "for the sake of preserving life." An ambulance arrived quickly. But the driver of the ambulance insisted on being paid immediately, in full, for his services. The Americans were all shocked with his insensitivity. Couldn't the Dean of the yeshiva be trusted to pay after the Sabbath was over? The driver was adamant, "Either full payment, or you drive him yourself to the hospital." Payment was made and the American students returned to their rooms that evening wondering if this hostility to religion was typical of secular Israelis.

SOL AND HIS friends, some of whom were his teammates on his high school varsity, decided to show their mettle to some of the secular Israelis kids. They challenged the local Hapoel basketball team to a match and defeated them. It was shocking for the Hapoel team to see religious yeshiva students, wearing *kipot*, skull-caps, more adept and aggressive in sports.

SOL RECALLED LIVING in a *tserif* [shack], while the permanent dorms were being constructed. Vegetables and fruit were plentiful, but meat was scarce - one teaspoonful for the Sabbath meal. There was plenty of jelly and bread, olives, tomatoes, eggplant and potatoes. He had to adjust to the idea; the main meal was at noon, while the evening meal was modest, consisting of bread and jelly, tea and a few olives.

The first few weeks in Rehovot were exciting and included trips, to the Galil and the Negev. Sol quickly picked up more Hebrew vocabulary, and it was thrilling for him to enter a restaurant and order food in Hebrew. The American students went native, dressing only in khaki shorts or trousers and wearing sandals without socks. Most of the streets in Rehovot were not paved and one walked on sand. Nearby, there was construction on the Weizmann Institute, the premier science research center. Much of Rehovot consisted of orange orchards and other agricultural sites. Sol loved the informality of daily life, the dress code, and the ubiquitous citrus scent from the groves.

But he had to leave the idyllic world of Rehovot to advance his studies for ordination in Jerusalem. The environment at Yeshivat Mercaz HaRav was fiercely Zionistic, unlike the other traditional yeshivas in Jerusalem. The students dressed in khaki clothes like Sabras. He sensed that they considered him no different than any other immigrant, and one ridiculed his foreign, American accent.

Vyse Avenue

"Why can't you speak Hebrew like a human being?" a student chided him. Sol was surprised that this student, a son of a Polish refugee, was belittling him. What *chutzpah!*

Could he be accepted as an authentic Israeli? Was *aliyah* possible? These questions resonated in the minds of all the Americans who had come with strong Zionist backgrounds and who became even more imbued by the élan of Israel. But could they sever their ties with family and friends for the sake of their Zionist ideals? In addition, what about their American roots?

Adela repeatedly reminded Sol how fortunate he was to be living in America, where there was safety from the Arabs, and the great opportunity of wealth. She lamented the austerity of Israeli life in comparison to her luxurious lifestyle in her native Lvov, which she still called, *Lemberg*. Most of all, she complained about the high taxes and the price of a decent dress or silk stockings. Her husband, Emil, had been a highly successful and esteemed photographer in Lvov with forty stores. In Israel, he had the photos of leading personalities, David Ben Gurion and Moshe Dayan, in his shop window. But photographic equipment was expensive, because of the import taxes. Fortunately, Sol had brought some film with him for a gift.

Sol marveled at Yula's spacious apartment. They set aside a room for him when he spent a week-end with them. Edik, Yula's husband, was very accommodating and often took Sol on trips in Israel.

Sol gave some of his "luxurious" items - his electric razor, nylon shirts and silk ties - to his relatives. Who would have thought that shoes or trousers were expensive? Sol was deeply impressed with their gratitude. His relatives treated him as an authentic American, not the child of immigrants. They never stopped reminding him that it was insane to contemplate *aliyah*.

SOL LAUGHED as he recalled this unexpected event when they arrived in Israel. One of the American students wrote his father that he loved his "homeland Israel," and was planning to stay and make aliyah. A series of phone calls raced back from New York to Rehovot. The father, a prominent Zionist leader and official of the Jewish Agency, and his wife, were deeply upset. Their seventeen year old son was too young to make such a rash decision. The Dean of the yeshiva extracted a promise from the student that he would return to New York after the year's study program and then decide, when he was older, to make aliyah. The entire incident was a scandal in the mind of the other Americans. Three years later, the parents succumbed to their son's idealistic plans and they followed him to Israel.

THURSDAY... Sol entered the office promptly, and waited a few minutes. The secretary then informed him that the Chief Rabbi was called to an important meeting in the north. Sol should come the following morning at 9:00 A.M. Sol was alarmed because Friday was the weekly gathering of all the local, fawning rabbis.

Sol returned to his room at the yeshiva and tried to rest. He had spent the entire previous day reflecting on his year's program in Israel and the hope of returning to America with *semicha* from the Chief Rabbi. He knew that his parents would call their relatives and friends. Mamma would call Rabbi Perlman with the joyous news.

Vyse Avenue

SOL WOULD BECOME independent. He would confront the Dean of the Brooklyn Mesivta, who spoke so contemptuously about his father. He would seek a pulpit and a doctoral program in Jewish history.

But what if he fails the test? Sol was apprehensive that his ten-year spiritual journey would be nullified. Nullified? Impossible! He would draw faith and courage from his mentor, Rabbi Fox, who inspired him in Hebrew School and led him on his road to Orthodoxy. He could not disappoint him!

SOL WONDERED; how did I endure the years of boring Talmud lectures?" Fortunately, the classes in the "secular" department in the afternoon included both Bible study and Modern Hebrew Literature. He was intellectually enriched by those afternoon Hebrew sessions with a young and dynamic teacher who went on to become one of the leading Hebrew educators of his era, winning the coveted "Israel Prize."

He was challenged by the Biblical stories of iconic personalities, men of flesh and blood, like Joshua, David and Samson, who manifested the full range of human emotions. He enjoyed reading Modern Hebrew Literature, which included works by Bialik, David Frischman and A.D. Gordon. These Hebrew poems, stories and essays spoke to his world and deepened his roots as a Jew, and his love of Hebrew and Israel.

In contrast, he knew nothing about the personal lives of the rabbis of the Talmud - Rav and Samuel, Rabba and Abaye. They were profound scholars, great minds, but

211

devoid of flesh and blood. Did they really exist, or were they the abstract constructs of the editors of the Talmud? How did they live? Why are there no detailed histories of their lives?

Most essential, for Sol's survival, was his passion for basketball!

SOL TURNED HIS THOUGHTS to his home in the Bronx, and read the letter from his friend, Stan, about the "Youth Minyan." It was also called, "The Young Adults Group" which held services at his synagogue. Since his Bar Mitzvah, Sol had joined a separate Sabbath morning service initiated by his friends, Murray, Albert and Mr. Dolney, who was their patron. Sol enjoyed attending with his friends where he could read the Torah and practice his cantorial skills. Above all, he felt a sense of belonging. They occupied the *Beth Hamedresh* [the basement vestry], of the synagogue on Sabbath mornings. This conflicted with some of the synagogue's adults who wished to use the vestry for their own needs - a Kiddush club, serving liquor and cake. In addition, the young men did not pay dues, and were seen by some of the adult elite as parasites. For most of the synagogue leadership, the Youth Service was a boon to the synagogue which had few young people.

On one Sabbath morning, one of the executives came down to the Young Adults Group with a view to deprecate their competence to conduct services themselves.

"Let's see if you boys know how to chant the service," he challenged.

Danny was sent up to the *bimah* to conduct the service and sang in a mellifluous tenor voice. He was far superior to any adult in the congregation. The executive was nonplussed at the excellent singing and retreated upstairs humiliated, amid the laughter of the youth. The other youth were also surprised at hearing Danny's superb tenor voice. No one knew that Danny had been receiving voice lessons in preparation to become a professional cantor. Within a short time, he was elected to be the cantor of a prestigious synagogue and a regular singer on radio's WEVD.

STAN'S LETTER related another confrontation, shortly thereafter, which dissolved the Young Adult's Service.

Dear Sol,

I enjoyed reading your last letter and hope to hear from you further about your studies. Most people were highly impressed with what you had to say regarding your advanced studies as compared to the United States.

Some highly dramatic and unbelievable incidents have taken place between the Young Adults Group and the synagogue. The executives demanded that the Young Adults be out of the synagogue by 11:00 A.M. Saturday morning, so that they can have their wine and cake. They tried to force them to relocate all the way upstairs, but Dulney and Co. refused.

The following Saturday morning, the executives were in the basement and blocked the *bimah* so that none of the young men could go up. A small kid was sent up to *daven* (a sacrifice), and they threw him off. Mr. Dulney and some of the older men protested, but in vain. After more resistance, the executives called the police. When the police arrived they were reluctant to intervene and asked if there were someone like a priest, who could settle this matter without the police. All looked at the rabbi, who remained silent.

A few days later, at a special meeting, the Young Adults voted to leave, roughly 12 to 8. Services are now conducted at the 174th St. synagogue on the hill where the group was welcomed with open arms. The decision appears to be irrevocable. Have you any suggestions or comments concerning this mess? Take care of your body and mind.

Your friend,

Stan

SOL BELIEVED that this angry confrontation was one of the reasons he chose to become a rabbi. He understood the special needs of young people. Albert, and a few others, felt disheartened. Sol was also disappointed, but understood that this was shul politics.

9:00 A.M. FRIDAY... When Sol entered the office, the Chief Rabbi was seated at his desk. Sol's test would be the first item on his crowded agenda. Following the test, he would permit the other rabbis to greet him. The Chief Rabbi asked in Hebrew, "Hebrew or Yiddish?" Sol, felt relieved. Thank God not in English. Sol chose Hebrew.

The test went quickly. The Chief Rabbi opened a number of texts from the small set of Talmud behind his desk, and asked fundamental questions and received the correct answers. The Chief Rabbi was very pleased. It seems that the Chief Rabbi selected questions from the texts that Sol knew and understood! A half-hour had passed and the

Chief Rabbi was satisfied that the candidate was well-qualified to be a rabbi.

He wrote a few sentences on a slip of paper and asked, "Do you wish to have your s*emicha* on a parchment written by a scribe *without* my signature, or on my official stationery *with* my personal signature." Sol answered, "I would prefer your personal signature on your stationery."

The secretary was called in to type the *semicha* certificate, after which, the Chief Rabbi affixed his signature and seal. The text included the decisive words declaring that, So Friedman,, the "outstanding Rav from New York has displayed knowledge of Talmud and Codes and was therefore granted permission, YOREH, YOREH, he may decide in matters of Torah." At last, Sol was ordained!

The ordeal was over. Sol hurried to a local photographer to make copies of his *semicha* and dashed off an aerogramme to his parents.

Dear Mamma and Daddy,
Good news. I passed my semicha test with the Chief Rabbi. You can tell the family and friends - will be coming home in June Love, Sol

Charles H. Freundlich

Vyse Avenue

FRAGMENTS

SOL SPENT MANY HOURS with Irene and Yula speaking about the quotidian aspects of life in America. "How much do dresses cost? How much is a Mix Master?"

They wondered, Sol was ordained, and will return to America; will we still hear from him? He is part of our family. They were amazed at the level of prosperity which the Friedmans enjoyed though they were immigrants. "America is the land of wealth and promise," Irene declared, and Yula affirmed.

"That's not what America is about," Sol responded. "What makes America great is that people have the opportunity and freedom to make choices. If they choose to

217

work hard and study, they will succeed and rise out of poverty. Adela asserted, "But you don't have high taxes and a bureaucracy that keeps people poor. Here, in Israel, we all struggle to make a living. How can we become rich?"

Sammy suggested, "Why don't you tell us about your family? How did they rise out of poverty? My grandfather Shmuel, whom I am named after, was your father's older brother. We have lost contact for many years."

"Tell us more about your life in America," said Yula. "Your family is part of our family."

"Sol responded "I feel the same way about you. My parents were immigrants, like you, who struggled, had to adjust, and succeeded in making a decent life. My parents were poor when they arrived from Europe; for many years, we remained on the fringe of poverty, and today, we are better off - not wealthy."

"You're not middle-class?" Adela asked. "How were you able to send us those very nice gifts of clothes?"

"You don't have to be rich to buy and share your clothes with family that survived the Holocaust," Sol replied.

Sol spent more than three hours relating his family's story and struggles, and found them intrigued. They were so excited in learning about the details of the Friedmans that they pressed Sol to write a brief history - even some brief fragments about his youth.

Sol agreed. The following day, he began to write some recollections, memories - mostly fragments about his youth.

FRAGMENTS OF MY YOUTH

MY EARLY YEARS were similar to other youth growing up during the 1940's. I loved baseball; sports dominated my youth. The Yankees with their superstars, Lou Gehrig and Joe DiMaggio, defeated the Chicago Cubs in the World's Series. In 1952, with the iconic Mickey Mantle, the Yankees captured the hearts of Bronx youth. I was a Giant fan, which rendered me and the few Dodger fans next door, as peculiar. This was a prescient decision, to break out of the mold and make my own personal way in life. Sometimes, we saved money to see a Yankee game at the Stadium or a Giants Football game at The Polo Grounds; but these treats were rare.

My parents owned a grocery store on Grand Avenue in the West Bronx for a few years, but like most businesses in the Depression, it failed. They next moved to a small apartment above a tax-payer in the Bensonhurst section of Brooklyn. After five years, they returned to The Bronx in 1938atrium and rented a commodious apartment at 1150 Vyse Avenue. It was an upward move, and the modern, impressive, red-brick building had two wings and an atrium. We lived on the ground floor, slightly above the sidewalk level, and needed only two steps to enter the hallway leading to our apartment. For my mother, obese and diabetic, this was most fortunate - like the other apartment buildings, it had no elevator.

The location was convenient, only four short blocks from two subway stations, and was a thirty-minute ride to Manhattan, where most people worked. Most important, it

219

meant a single fare of a nickel. The apartment was luxurious by my parent's standards, and included a Frigidaire, gas stove, steam heat and running hot water. Across the hallway, was a storage room which had space for carriages, a public pay phone, and a pay washing machine. Next to the storage room, lived the hard-working Polish Superintendent with whom my mother could chat in his native tongue. With two bedrooms, an eat-in kitchen, a toilet with a shower in the bathtub, and a large living room, for the six of us - could one have imagined a more idyllic home?

For the youth, the highlights of The Bronx were: The Boulevard, The Loew's Paradise, Alexander's Department Store, Krum's Ice Cream Parlor, The Grand Concourse, and Orchard Beach. For my parents, the main attraction was the Jennings Street food market, with its outdoor stands, where you could purchase farm-fresh produce; kosher meat and chicken at reduced prices, and sour pickles straight out of the barrel from "Jake the Pickle man." (Tragically, Jake made the headlines,when he was murdered in 1960 during a robbery).

The food vendors would shout while hawking, "Tomatoes, five cents a pound, five cents a pound. Come and get it." These were the war years, and though my father was working, the family was living on the edge of poverty. However, so many people were in dire economic straits that we never felt poor or deprived.

The half-hour subway trip from the Bronx to Manhattan was a nickel, and we often visited the city museums which had no admission charge. God bless Mrs. Kaplan, our fifth grade teacher in P.S. 66, who insisted that we, the children of immigrants, acquire culture by visiting the great Metropolitan Museum of Art and the Museum of Natural History. On Mondays, she would quiz us about our visits, and admonish those who failed to go. There were no school buses and we all walked to the neighborhood public schools, which served more than a million pupils throughout The Bronx.

There were six apartment buildings, all six stories high, on one side of Vyse Avenue, and each was a different color brick. The kids in one building formed their own social clique or sports club, and often disassociated with the other kids. Since we lived on the ground level; and our windows were barely five feet above the sidewalk, we sometimes climbed in through the front window of our apartment, instead of entering through the front door.

It was remarkable that during the nineteen years we lived there, no burglar ever attempted to break into our home. Perhaps it was because our windows faced the street and the brownstones, where more than one hundred families lived in close quarters. In those brownstones, directly facing our apartment, there lived some tightly-knit Italian families. One didn't dare antagonize anyone from these closely-knit clans; the men were tough, strong, and muscular.

My mother was very congenial and gregarious, always smiling, with a sense of humor, open to the neighbors and always offering to do a favor. An immigrant from a *shtetl* in the Galician area of Austria-Hungary (later Poland then Ukraine), she nursed her ethnic prejudices. But she was very affable to all, especially to our Polish superintendent, the Italian neighbors across the street, and the Irish tenants who lived in our building. She spoke derisively about the *prust,* common, poor Jewish immigrants from Russia. She

221

was distressed to learn that one of my closest friends, who lived in the next building, was the son of a cab-driver, whom she called a *bal agalah.* Her *shtetl* had a rigid class system; the "better Jews" did not associate, or even worship in the same *shuls,* as the tailors, shoemakers, or wagon drivers. However, America modified many of her Old World attitudes.

We all lived close to each other and had to be neighborly, even if privately, we had our prejudices. Perhaps it was because most of the adults were immigrants. There were few WASPS who spoke unaccented English who could remind us that we were tolerated guests - not real Americans.

We felt safe and secure among the diverse ethnic groups because Mamma was always home. None of the kids in our family had a key to the apartment. If Mamma was out shopping, we climbed into our apartment from the back alley, and through the kitchen window, which was not locked. In the alley, we cultivated a close friendship with many alley cats and kept a few for our pets. We named one *Tova Lieba*, after Mamma's sister, who perished in the Holocaust.

We did not own a car. In fact, there were not more than three cars parked on Vyse Avenue; with little traffic, we were able to play in the street without fear. Without a car, how did we shop for food? Most of us had small Frigidaires (some only had ice-boxes) with no freezer compartments. When we purchased food, it was sufficient for the day. Mamma was very frugal, and walked the four blocks to Jennings Street, pushing a baby carriage, to obtain a larger load of produce, milk and other dairy foods to save a few pennies. Others, more socially conscious, owned carts with large wheels, to transport their purchases. The more affluent had food delivered from the local grocer.

The apartments in the three-story brownstones on the opposite side of the street, had more than six rooms, and the ground floor included a backyard. One of my friends lived on the ground floor, and we often played in his backyard. Another backyard belonged to "Uncle Louie," who built a *Sukkah* for the holiday, and invited all the children of the block, both Jewish and non-Jewish, for refreshments.

The apartments on our side of the street had three or four rooms. My younger brother slept on a folding bed in the large bedroom, next to my parents. My older brother and I slept in the smaller bedroom; my sister slept on a high-riser in the living room. We had comfortable, basic furniture; a private telephone and television came years later. We had one radio which was placed close to the large bedroom, and had to be set on the highest volume to accommodate all of us. We often heard the shout, "louder, I can't hear."

Mamma took pride in some of our furnishings: her living room rug by *Karastan*, two Chinese vase lamps, and a sofa with an Italian, hand-carved, frame. These modest furnishings were important to Mamma and were a testament to her once prominent family in her *shtetl*, Hustechko, (which she pronounced, Istichka). The two vase lamps were nestled on two round mahogany side tables with delicate carved borders. Very often we played *Black-Out,* knocked down the tables, and broke the delicate wooden borders. When Mamma came home and discovered the damage, she let loose with a torrent of screaming, took hold of a dish-towel - her weapon of choice - and began swinging at us. No one ever was injured from Mamma's attack. Her bark was worse than her bite; but it intimidated us and lowered her high blood pressure for the moment.

Mamma was the matriarch of the family and she bore the heritage of a lost pedigree stemming from her grandfather, Huna, an affluent landlord in her *shtetl*. We always had two sets of fine silverware (not sterling), and hand-sewn table-cloths because she still fancied herself part of the *shtetl* privileged class. Mamma never adjusted to the democratic-American ideal of status based on achievement and money - not pedigree or Torah learning. She continued to look with disdain and a little jealousy, on the nouveau riche in her *landsmanschaft,* (shtetl burial society), who were former tailors and shoe makers.

My father, Louis, was very affable, and radiated love. Everyone was enamored with his honesty and childlike personality. He was barely able to support his family, though he worked hard. Born to his father, Moshe Yosef, in his old age, he was the baby of the family. His sister, Miriam, and brother, Nuta, who lived close by, doted on him. He was deeply religious, donning *tallis and tefillin* every morning, offering a blessing before eating bread, and never ate without a hat. When he arrived home after work, he immediately chanted the daily evening prayers before dinner. He was my first tutor in my journey to religious faith.

Louis arose every morning at 4:30 A.M., for his job in Long Island City that required a one and a half hour train ride. He donned his *tefillin,* and quickly chanted the morning prayers. Then, he prepared a fresh brew of coffee, drank more than six cups, and smoked a few cigarettes, while reading the morning Yiddish newspaper. It was dark and serene; the family was asleep. These moments of reverie and solitude were a respite from the stress and insecurity of living with the stress of poverty. The routine morning schedule brought meaning and purpose to his life.

My mother had a tougher disposition, and rode the waves of stress and uncertainty with great aplomb. She was obese, hot-tempered - a result of her high blood pressure and diabetes - but always in control. She was able to handle the daily crises; the burden of the family's survival rested on her shoulders.

Much of our family aggravation revolved around the one small bathroom shared by the six of us. Early morning was a race to the bathroom. My sister, Elaine, monopolized it getting dressed and "putting on her face." My brothers and I had to contain our water as we screamed, "hurry up," and banged on the door in vain. But when Mamma had to get in, she shrieked, "I have a cramp. I have to go in. I'll make on the floor," the bathroom was vacated immediately. Our daily morning routine was accompanied by the radio's *John Gambling Show* which aired short classical pieces of music, and announced the time every five minutes. None of us owned a wrist-watch.

Mamma was astute in running the household finances. She had clever ways for earning extra money when not operating a bakery or grocery. She knitted doilies, men's skull-caps, or sold eggs, which she bought wholesale from a *landsman* in Manhattan. One of her unfortunate attempts to raise additional funds was renting to a border, who added to our cramped living quarters. Mamma brought in an elderly woman as a border to live in the small bedroom for ten dollars a month, and we all resented her invasion of our apartment. We were rude to her and she exclaimed, "No back talk." We named her, "No back talk," and she lasted only three months.

Summer vacations presented a challenge to most of us. We could not afford sleep-over or day camps, or a bungalow in the Catskills or Far Rockaway. During the hot summer months, before air-conditioners, we used to listen to the baseball games outdoors on radio. One kid, Stanley, had a portable radio, which ran on batteries. We would gather on his stoop by the white-bricked apartment building, on Vyse Avenue, next to Levine's Drug Store. He felt so prominent with his portable radio and he commanded our respect.

During the summers, when most of us remained in the city, we worked part-time. Some kids sold newspapers, shined shoes or, like me, worked as a soda-jerk in a candy store in the Hunts Point section of the Bronx. We often went to the beach in Coney Island on Sundays. It was a one-fare ride by subway that lasted an hour. Orchard Beach, in the Bronx, was closer - only a half-hour ride - but getting there required double carfare, subway and bus. By the time I was fifteen, I was able to walk to Orchard Beach from the last subway station, Pelham Bay Park, and it became my regular destination.

I often reflect, with amazement, how the saving of a nickel carfare shaped my lifestyle. Indeed, Mamma would send us four blocks to the Jennings Street market to buy a bottle of milk to save two cents rather than to the grocery store around the corner. This discipline enabled us to survive on our sparse budget. I never considered myself deprived or poor, but learning to be frugal - to save every penny - would benefit me, when I became a family man.

Vyse Avenue

We lived three blocks from *The Boulevard*, which consisted of two long streets on Southern Boulevard from Westchester Avenue to 163rd street. It was a fantasy land filled with numerous stores, and three movie theaters. Our apartment was cramped and we found diversion and escape by walking on the Boulevard, window shopping, and dreaming of possessing some of the toys and games. The Boulevard was our vision of Elysium, especially in the evening: when the neon lights glowed from the Toy Store, the Jewelry shops, the large display windows of *Ripley's* and *Crawford's Clothing*, *Vim's* and *Davega* sports stores, and the marquees of the three cinemas.

On the next block, *The Art Theater* featured foreign films. We often attended the *Freeman Theater*, on the corner of Freeman Street, which screened the latest films at a lower price, a few weeks after the more upscale theaters on the Boulevard. The cinemas would have a double feature, except for the *Star* - which screened three films.

We spent much play-time in the streets, which were safe and spacious. There were no parks nearby, and *Crotona Park* with its beautiful *Indian Lake* (for boating), handball, and basketball courts - was a mile's distance away. Indian Lake served as the venue for the annual Rosh Hashanah ritual, *tashlich,* when thousands of Jews from East and West Bronx gathered to "hurl their sins into the depths of the seas." It was also the favorite gathering place for Orthodox Jewish youth to socialize during the spring and summer months when the Sabbaths were long, and there were limited options for recreation. The benches around the lake were ideal for sitting, schmoozing, discussing politics, and making plans for Saturday evenings.

Across the street, on Crotona Park East, stood the prestigious *Kehilath Israel Synagogue*, where young Zionists of the *Shomer Hadati* held their meetings, danced, sang and made plans for *aliyah*, settling in the new state of Israel. A number of the members settled in *kibbutzim* after completing high school.

The Bronx Zoo was more than a mile's distance from our home, but we often attended on week-ends, when there was no admission charge. Van Cortland Park, one of the largest in the Bronx, was located in the north-western section, but had no direct public transportation. We heard about the terrific paddle-ball courts and games held there. We counted our time for play in the minutes. Some of us went to afternoon Hebrew School for an hour, and this disrupted our play schedule.

Our parents did not supervise our afternoon play and we devised many games using the walls of the buildings: *Stoop-ball*, throwing a Spalding against the steps of the brownstone stoops, *Walls,* which was played in the alley-way and *Johnny On The Pony*, which displayed the strength of the defensive team of five to support another five kids jumping on their backs.

We played cards, including Pinochle, Casino and Rummy, on the sidewalks, without any money or betting. Other popular games were: *Kick-ball,* with a rolled up newspaper, *Kick the Can*, and *Ring a levio* which was a game of tag.

The dominant game was *Stickball* (baseball, played with a broomstick and Spalding). There was also a small group that enjoyed hockey. Stanley used to play hockey on his roller-skates and the rest of us on foot. On Sundays, we hockey fans would often go to Madison Square Garden to watch the New York Rovers (with free tickets).

When World War II was over, we all celebrated with block parties, which included parades, drinking and refreshments. Each block had its own victory flag crossing the width of the street. Prosperity arrived, and people began buying cars, parking them on the streets, and many of our games were eliminated. Our local play area was diminished and we were compelled to travel to the playgrounds and schoolyards to play *Softball* and *Touch Football.*

One of the benefits of playing on the street was the fact that our parents knew where we were. Often a mother would look out the window and shout, "Marvin come home. It's time for dinner." Needless to say, Moms were home most of the time and Dads, who were expected to support their families, came home late.

Most of the adults in the Bronx were immigrants who spoke Yiddish, Polish or Italian. Many of the Irish were second and third generation Americans, who spoke a proper English, and were devoted to the Catholic Church. Their children attended St. John's Catholic School on Hoe Avenue; though many Italian Catholics attended the public schools with the Jewish children. Despite the socializing on the streets and school, intermarriage between Jews and non-Jews was deemed abhorrent. Among my closest friends were my classmates; James, an Italian, and Freddy who lived in the next building and Buddy, in my building. Heshy, another older teenager, was my pal.

Vyse Avenue was highly segregated; there were neither African-Americans (then called Negroes) or Hispanics living in the tenements. The only African-

American was Mr. Matthews, called, "Whitey", the superintendent of the brown apartment building, who guarded the alley from being utilized as a play area. We were terrified of the muscular Mr. Matthews who often scowled at the kids, but was very kind-hearted and accommodating to the adults. The White adults expressed fear and alarm as Blacks and Hispanics made their way up from Harlem and the South Bronx and moved into our neighborhood. Thus began the mass exodus to the West Bronx, Pelham Parkway and Long Island.

I loved attending public school (P.S. 66), with my own space, chair, desk and structured life. I adored every one of my teachers, respected them, and developed a high regard for education. I thought that I would become a teacher when I grew up. I did well in public school, and at my graduation, the principal, Mr. Sussman, praised me as a top student (though the Roosevelt Medal was given to another student who was tied with me). My mother didn't attend my graduation; she was too preoccupied with the daily struggle to survive. But an Italian neighbor, Mrs. Manzi, who attended, came to our front window, where Mamma was planted, to report the exciting news of my achievement. A few streets in our neighborhood were named after poets - Bryant and Longfellow. I never found out who "Vyse" was.

This was my world, the world of my youth, which nurtured my hopes and dreams to live a more prosperous life. When the neighborhood deteriorated with violent crime, and dirty streets, it was time to move. We looked confidently to our new apartment on Findlay Avenue, in the West Bronx. I believe that the many years I spent on Vyse Avenue were happy, and prepared me to face life with courage and optimism.

AFTER CONCLUDING the first chapter of the memoirs of his youth in the Bronx, Sol returned to his Israeli relatives. He explained his personal feelings about his dual-identity as an American and a Jew, whose religious roots are in Israel. He treasured both identities that added depth and value to his life.

"You see, we were once poor, struggled, worked hard, went to school, and made a decent life for ourselves. That's the American dream - not riches - but opportunity. It's only seven years since Israel became independent. You were fortunate to escape from Poland before the Holocaust. You fought bravely in the War for Independence, and we are all proud of you and Israel's achievements.

"I was thrilled to visit the Hebrew University, The Technion, the Weizmann Institute and Bar Ilan University. With such outstanding institutions of learning, Israel will grow, prosper and be a trail blazer in technology, and science, and an exemplar to the world. Israel will be a source of honor, pride and hope to the Jews in the Diaspora. I know I'll return; this year has been my *homecoming*."

They all hugged Sol, and Adela said, "The family will miss you. We know you will come home to us again."

Charles H. Freundlich

INGATHERING

GITTEL SPENT HOURS in the small kitchen fussing over the chickens, especially, the stuffing made with corn flakes. She fried the potato *kugel* on the stove (rather than bake it in the oven), and topped the honey cake with walnuts. The Hanukkah candles had been lit by Louis with the singing of the holiday melodies by the family, and the meal was shortly to begin. Gittel was pensive:

THE BOYS are home from Korea, Elaine and Max have come from Jersey with the grandchildren, Sol, has started teaching, and Louis is feeling much better after his operation. What more could she have wished for on this cool Sunday of Hanukkah?

Charles H. Freundlich

If only her father could see her now. How long has it been? She left Hustechko in 1919, when she was 18. Now, aged fifty-six, she was a wife, mother and grandmother. Was it right for her father to compel her to leave their home and immigrate to America all alone? But, he explained, there was no money for her dowry. Without a dowry, there would be no suitable husband for her. It was a terrible scandal, a disgrace, to marry a common worker.

It was a frightening challenge for her. She had little money, did not know the English language, and had no higher education or skills. What she had was a Tante, her mother's sister, who had immigrated to America and settled in New York's Lower East Side five years earlier, and established a clothing shop. Her aunt would take care of her, give her work and let her live in the back of the shop.

Her father, Avram Abba, would be so proud of her now. She could speak English, had managed a grocery and bakery for a number of years and had a lovely apartment - with an indoor toilet! How wonderful it was to have an indoor toilet with plumbing, instead of the odoriferous out-house which was unpleasant during the winters. How fortunate she was in marrying Louis; kind, hard-working, and honest, who never criticized her, never complained, and never used vulgar language. Louis upheld the traditions of her family, prayed every morning with *tallis and tefillin,* and shared the same values. He had gone through a serious operation and, thank God, he was much better and ready to retire. The monthly Social Security benefits would offer stability and contentment to her stressful life.

Vyse Avenue

GITTEL INVITED Breina to join them in the family meal. She still lived in the brownstone across the street, and maintained the *shtiebel* in her father's memory. In addition, Gittel invited Arnold and his wife, Irene. How splendid things worked out for them, praise God, after his wife died and her husband was killed in an accident in the army.

Gittel knew how to manage all thirteen for dinner in the living room cum dining room. It was a tribute to her ingenuity, having catered her three sons' Bar Mitzvah luncheons in the same apartment. Her present challenge to seat thirteen at the dining room table with two added leaves was facile.

"Elaine, come see the chickens. Are they brown enough?" Gittel shouted from the kitchen. Since her marriage, Elaine, (who had never boiled an egg prior to her marriage), had acquired the fine art of haute cuisine - special thanks to her Hungarian mother-in-law, who was most solicitous that her Max not starve to death at the hands of this *inexperienced American bride from the Bronx, who took her son away.*

LOUIS WAS taciturn and felt cheerful among the guests for having to begin the meal with the *motzi*, the opening blessing. It was sufficient that his children were safe, educated and self-reliant - no evil eye. Hardly four months had passed since the operation on his colon, which proved to be a success. But he was sixty-four, well past the age when his own parents passed away, and he could look forward to receiving his Social Security checks. In addition to their modest savings (thanks to Gittel's handling of the finances), it would provide them with a modest but respectable living standard. Above all, he would be finished with the arduous treks to work prior to day-break during the bitter winters. Gone was the unrelenting fear of insufficient money to pay the rent.

He would be able to take an honorable seat at shul, perhaps, give an occasional donation for an *aliyah*, and even attend daily minyan. He would often mention to his rabbi, that his son had been ordained by the Chief Rabbi of Israel. The rabbi would praise Louis for raising such a religious boy in an age when most Jewish youth were rebelling against the tradition. Louis' father, of blessed memory, resting in the Tolner Hassidim section of Baron Hirsch Cemetery in Staten Island, would be proud of him, the son of his old age. His long odyssey from uprooted refugee to naturalized citizen was over. His life was full of miracles, he reflected, on this Hanukkah.

"COMING IN with the soup," Gittel announced while lugging in a large white tureen that Elaine presented to her on Mother's Day.

"Let me help, Mom," Elaine said.

"Sit, today you are my guest. But if you insist, you can help by serving Max and the children."

"I'll also help," added Irene.

The meal proceeded slowly, and predictably with soup, roast chicken, stuffing, apple sauce (Gittel didn't like cranberries), sweet potatoes, honey cake and tea. Nothing extraordinary, but it was the sameness of the festive meal each Hanukkah, that provided comfort to Gittel's life especially, when the whole family was together for the first time in years.

Louis made an announcement, "Before we *bentch,* [say grace], let's all spend a few minutes talking about the miracles on this Hanukkah.

"Splendid idea, Daddy," Elaine responded. "This is our first Hanukkah dinner together in years."

"I'm thankful that the boys are home from Korea, safe and sound," Gittel proclaimed. "That's enough miracles for me."

"I think there are many other things to be thankful - like Daddy's successful operation," Elaine added.

"And what about Sol's receiving *semicha* from the Chief Rabbinate," Louis chimed.

"And what about my new job at American Auto," Marvin boasted.

"And what about my acceptance into Brooklyn College for matriculation," Seymour added.

"Let's all chat a while about our dreams that have come true," Louis said.

"I have an announcement," said Breina. "I'm going back to school, to City College, and will be majoring in social work. I always wanted to help people, especially since my father passed away."

"That's wonderful, *mazel tov,* " Gittel responded.

"I've been seeing a psychologist the past five months and he has helped me greatly," Breina continued. "I was miserable. I couldn't continue mourning for my father, of blessed memory, and I had to make a change. I feel I must continue to keep up the shul, but I have to make a life of my own. I have another happy announcement. I've met a wonderful boy in school. I like him and I think he likes me, too. He's modern Orthodox, a graduate of Yeshiva College, and is studying for his master's degree at Columbia."

The Friedmans were astonished, but delighted, with the transformation in Breina's life. She had emerged from her chrysalis of delusions to engage the real world of opportunity.

"I have an announcement," said Irene. "I'm expecting in June. In fact, we are looking for a larger apartment with another bedroom. If it's a girl we will name her after Arnold's wife, who died so young. We'll be leaving Vyse Avenue soon."

"Mazel Tov," declared Elaine, (who had just passed her second monthly, and was praying that it would be a girl). But she was too cautious to say anything; even Max did not know.

ELAINE CLOSED HER EYES and smelled the luscious aroma of roast chicken and fried potatoes. She reflected on the passing years.

As the oldest child, she had borne the brunt of the family's poverty during the Depression - though President Roosevelt had inspired relief and hope for the future. Her fantasies of becoming a concert pianist and marrying a wealthy socialite were dissipated. She was adjusted to the small-town life in Jersey. Life was uneventful, but stable, predictable and secure - that was her happiness. She loved her husband and children.

Above all, she had triumphed over the failed romances in her life. There was Jerry, an army veteran, who worked in his father's upscale bakery in Forest Hills, Long Island. Jerry was vivacious, warm and generous. When he came for Elaine on Saturday evenings, he never brought less than three rich layer cakes, an assortment of onion rolls, bagels, éclairs and Napoleons. The boys had a feast and prayed that Jerry would be their brother-in-law.

Jerry had no misgivings about Elaine. But his parents, conscious of their own laborious struggle to achieve middle-class respectability, realized - Elaine would not fit in with their circle. Jerry's family, were successful merchants, though lacking much in haute couture and refinement. Their business prospered, they had money, and they considered themselves upper middle-class, and well-established in the community.

Elaine's family, they felt, were nice but common, with the odor of garlic - poor immigrants without class. Jerry argued with his parents, but gave in to their persistent pressure. Gittel had not grasped the truth - in America, status is based on money. Gittel's braggadocio of her family's high social status in the shtetl meant nothing to Jerry's parents.

The next romance was Maurice. He was polished, well-dressed, had a subtle Hungarian accent, and captured the heart of Elaine, who had been depressed for more than a month.

However, Elaine's desire to start a family and Maurice's modest income led to sharp disagreements, and the engagement was broken off. Gittel cursed, "Those Hungarians are bloodsuckers. May they both suffer a stroke!"

Many of Elaine's girlfriends were already engaged or married, and she felt like a misfit. What was wrong with her? Nothing – except money!

Then, her luck began to change. Max came to visit his sister, Marsha, who lived on the floor above the Friedmans. Between Marsha, whose maiden name was also Friedman, and Gittel - a match was arranged.

"I always admired the Hungarian Jews, so refined and respectable," Gittel exclaimed.

ELAINE REFLECTED, how clearly I remember when our home was custom built, (according to Max' specifications) with almost 3,000 square feet. My two boys, one year apart, are full of life, boisterous and healthy; I pray that my next child will be a girl. I achieved my deepest yearnings to be a wife and mother, secure financially, and a source of pride to my parents. I have triumphed over the local white trash on Vyse Avenue that disparaged my looks and dress, and especially, my modesty.

"YOU KNOW WHAT Daddy?" Elaine began, "I remember the green velvet dress you and Mamma bought me for my Sweet Sixteen party, the one with the bow in front. It was a hit with my girlfriends. From then on, I knew I would make it socially. Louise, my best friend, complimented me and said that I looked like a movie star."

"You were always beautiful from the day you were born," Louis smiled.

"What do you think, Seymour?" Louis asked.

SEYMOUR REFLECTED on his challenges and victories:

He had returned from Korea with a passion to return to college and attain a good life. He struggled through

Monroe High School with a "B" average and a General Diploma, not suitable for City College, but adequate for non-matriculation at Brooklyn College. This meant a long *shlep* on the subway from the Bronx; but he had worked in Coney Island and was used to commuting. He had a seat both ways and could do most of his reading assignments on the train.

He had registered for evening courses as a non-matriculated freshman among younger students who had not served in the Military, and he found it difficult to compete with them. During the day, he found work in a clothing store on Wilkins Avenue, and this was sufficient to cover his personal needs, and to help out with the family's expenses. He took pride and satisfaction that he was independent, on his way to a career.

In Korea, he had served his country, was proud to be an American veteran, and his self-esteem was greatly enhanced. He was confident and ready to take his place in a competitive society.

He thought that he would go into teaching, a realistic and practical vocation for many men in New York City. It paid fairly well, offered excellent benefits, health coverage, early retirement, and required little risk or challenge of failure. But he was not proficient in writing. He reflected, my athletic abilities should make me suitable to be a gym teacher and perhaps a basketball coach. I love basketball, though track was my specialty.

SEYMOUR RESPONDED, "My first goal is to get my B.A. and go into teaching. The world opens up for you when you have a good educational background."

"And what do you have to say, Marvin?" Gittel asked.

MARVIN WAS a disappointment to Gittel. He chose to attend Gompers Vocational High School in order to study auto-mechanics, rather than preparing for college. It was aggravating for Gittel to believe that her son, a Jewish boy, is throwing away an opportunity for a free education at City College. Marvin was bright and intelligent. How unfortunate, to work with his hands like a peasant!

Gittel recalled her older brother, Moishe, of blessed memory, who aspired to attend a Technological School in Lemberg, and the bribes which her grandfather, Huna, had to pay.A heartbreak, that her son should throw away this opportunity to be a professional and well- respected.

MARVIN REFLECTED about his choices:

Gittel did not appreciate my feelings. I love working with my hands, making real things. It was not that I was stupid or indolent but rather my desire to make things: model planes, wooden toys, and decorative ash-trays, that provided me a sense of joy and satisfaction. I enjoy using my hands and sweating over a project. It was my life to enjoy and if Gittel and Louis did not understand my values and desires - that was their problem. I am determined not to go to college, nor would I take the academic courses in Vocational High School that would enable me to have a choice! I made my choice - an expert auto-mechanic, working for American Auto Repairs!

I love cars and peering into the complex parts under the hood. I will have security and a promise of an excellent pension program with health insurance for the rest of my life. Of course, not being a professional, limits my social opportunities for dating. Most Jewish girls were snobs and would not go out with me. Gittel had mentioned her *landsman*, a second cousin from Hustechko, the one with a dry-goods store on the Lower East Side, who had a daughter. But I was not going to be fixed up by Mamma. Gittel was insistent, "There's a good dowry with their only daughter."

MARVIN had little success with his dates and he began listening to his mother's suggestions. He might even give that girl on the Lower East Side a call.

He began his litany of gratitude:

"I'm happy to be home from Korea and grateful to be back with the family. I'm working steady, own my own car and feel good about myself. I'm glad to be with you, Daddy and Mamma, and eagerly looked forward to your letters you sent me when I was in Korea. It was rough and cold in Korea and I felt restless in the sleeping bags. I felt like I was choking, gasping for breath. Now I feel comfortable in my folding bed near the window. It's good to be home."

"What about you, Sol? Gittel queried.

SOL RETURNED HOME jubilant. He succeeded in attaining his ordination, but was indecisive about his future. He was twenty-two - too young to marry, and too inexperienced to seek a pulpit. He loved learning, especially Jewish history and Modern Hebrew literature, but knew that a rabbi's status depended on his expertise in the classic texts of Bible and Talmud.

He recalled his excitement during his reading of Graetz's "History of the Jews," an illuminating and transformative experience. For the first time, he grasped the reality that Judaism was alive, more than ancient texts to be analyzed and obeyed. He believed the Jewish people to be special, chosen by God, and he longed to study and add to the chain of tradition. He planned to enroll in the Bernard Revel Graduate School of Yeshiva University for his doctorate. He would teach at Hebrew School during the afternoons, and attend classes during the mornings. This would enable him to be financially independent and also to contribute some money to his parents.

He had begun dating, but his lack of savings and a steady job, put marriage on the slow burner. Some girls dropped him when they realized he was not ready to commit.

SOL BEGAN joyfully:

"I'm grateful for studying in Israel and being ordained. I'm thankful for returning safely to the Bronx with all of you. I feel I have two homes - America and Israel. I know that part of me, my soul, is still there. I have always felt at home in the Bronx with its large Jewish population, more than a half-million, many of them still deeply rooted in the Old Country.

"But Israel is something new and special, beyond the imagination - Israel is the future. Only in Israel, is Hebrew, the language of the Bible, spoken. The streets are named after Jewish heroes, and the Jewish holidays are the national holidays; Shabbat is the normal day of rest. The very air you breathe is Jewish, and you feel authentically Jewish. There's no shame in flaunting your Jewishness in public and the boys wear a knitted *kippa* in the street rather an unobtrusive hat. The policemen and the soldiers are Jewish and you feel secure, and unafraid. Where else can you sense the vibrant spirit of Judaism? I know that I will return; perhaps not to live permanently, but certainly to visit. I will return often, to refresh my Jewish soul and to reconnect with our family there."

"Bravo, bravo," Louis exclaimed. "Spoken like a true Zionist."

Seymour objected, "But what about your American roots? Aren't you still proud to be an American?"

"I certainly am, and I rediscovered some of the best things about America, its democracy and opportunity - by living abroad. But Israel is catching up. Everywhere, there is construction, growth, and thousands of new immigrants from the four corners of the earth. Believe me - this is the beginning of the Messianic age - Israel is the future for all the Jewish people."

"You don't have to convince us, Sol," responded Gittel. "We have all your letters from Israel, every one of them, filled with your joy and excitement. We are all happy that there was no war with Egypt while you were there. Welcome home, Rabbi Friedman."

"Do our relatives want to stay in Israel? I mean with the Arabs always threatening war, how do they live?" Elaine asked.

"I think they'll stay. After all, it took years, after returning from Poland and Central Asia, to establish themselves. By Israeli standards, they're okay. And they have a decent apartment with a garden in the back and a Jeep. They'll stay and grow with the young nation."

"I understand that my Aunt Leah's son-in-law is a big shot in Rishon," Gittel added.

"That's true. I also visited the Rudnicks, your cousins, in Haifa and they're very fine people. Mr. Rudnick is an accountant and he remembers your grandfather, Huna. They treated me very well. They left Hustechko before the war and he spent seven years in England before coming to Israel. His English was perfect and I enjoyed chatting with him."

"Do you think they'll need auto-mechanics in Israel?" asked Marvin. "Maybe I'll visit."

"I think I'd like to go with you," added Seymour.

"I'm happy and content to be in Jersey," Max exclaimed. "I've had enough traveling from Hungary to America. I wouldn't want to be an immigrant again. It took me years to settle down and start a successful business. I don't want to start all over again."

"Perhaps it would not be good for you, Max. But you would miss out if you didn't make at least one visit," Sol responded.

"I think it's time to finish eating the honey cake and *bentch*," said Louis.

Following the Grace, Gittel stood up. "I have an important announcement to make. Everyone, please listen. You remember what happened last month when I opened the door and there were kids fighting in the hall? Louis and I had enough of this neighborhood and we decided we are going to move. Nineteen years on Vyse Avenue are enough. You know how hard it is to find an apartment today with the rents so high. But, to my *mazel*, who did I bump into on Jennings Street? It was our friend Mrs. Brodsky whose husband used to supply our grocery store on Grand Avenue. Well, I greeted her and she was so happy to meet me. She's the one who has the very smart daughter, Anne, who graduated Hunter College. And yes, she's the one who bought us a crib for a present when Elaine was born. Guess what - I tell her we want to move.

She says, "I have an apartment building in the West Bronx."

I ask, "How much is the rent?"

She says, "Don't worry, it's rent-controlled."

I say, "How large?"

She says, "It's very large, beautiful and modern. It has casement windows, a sunken living room and parquet floors. It has an eat-in kitchen with a foyer."

"Well, to make a long story short, Louis and I visited the apartment on Findlay Avenue in the West Bronx, off the Concourse, and it was beautiful. It was on the fifth floor, but there's an elevator, and the living room windows have a beautiful view of the park. It was too good to be true and we didn't know for sure when the tenants were moving. Last night, Mrs. Brodsky called us. We can have the apartment in two months."

"Thank God, we are moving," Seymour said.

"Thank God, we are going to a beautiful apartment which we can afford. I know that you boys will be leaving soon and be getting married. Louis will be collecting Social Security next year, and we will be able to afford the rent without your help"

"Mom, we'll always be helping out," said Elaine.

"You can always count on us," added Seymour, who was working full-time.

"I'll miss Vyse Avenue," Marvin lamented.

"Nineteen years is enough. It's time to move on," said Seymour.

"I'll miss Jennings Street and our neighbors," Gittel reflected.

"I have a car, Mom," said Marvin. "I'll drive you there anytime you want. I'll miss the guys on the block."

"My classmates and the Orthodox guys from *shul* are my friends, I feel no attachment to the guys on Vyse Avenue," said Sol.

Seymour responded, "What guys? Most of our neighbors already have moved out to the West Bronx, Pelham Parkway or the Island. There is no one left. We are the Last of the Mohicans."

"True," lamented Gittel. "Our neighbors have already moved."

"I don't remember any other place but Vyse Avenue," noted Marvin. "I was three when we came from Brooklyn. I have many close friends here. I'll try to keep in touch."

Elaine interjected, "I've been living in Jersey for the last six years and I miss the family, not the street. Your home is where your family is. I know you'll all be happy in your new apartment."

Max added, "My sister, Marsha moved to Yonkers, last year; bought a beautiful home, and she doesn't miss Vyse Avenue."

"I loved living on Vyse Avenue," Louis exclaimed. "My family lived close by. Nuta, of blessed memory, lived on Simpson Street, and Miriam and John were close by on Southern Boulevard, until they moved to Brooklyn. And there was my uncle who had the Army and Navy store on the corner of 167th street. I felt at home here."

Gittel added, "Today, everyone moves. Families don't live in the same neighborhood. Children move away to get jobs and leave their parents' home. It's a new world. Believe it or not, my father, Avram Abba, and grandfather, Huna, and many generations going back, were born and lived in the same Hustechko. We never moved and our cemetery has gravestones more than three hundred years old."

"But we have telephones - families can stick together," Elaine argued. "I live more than a hundred miles away, and I call almost every day, right, Mom?"

Gittel lamented, "What are nineteen years in my family memories?" You were all little children when we came. Now you've grown up. You'll all get married and move away, like Elaine."

"Mom, you forget how you moved away from your family in Hustechko when you were eighteen," Seymour noted.

"Moved away - that's a laugh. I ran away from poverty, from war, from a miserable life with no future. I had no choice. I left without my family. I was alone, living with my Tante for five years until I got married."

"Let's not talk about the past," Louis interjected. "The past is over. I don't ever talk about the time we ran away from Bukovina. My father had lost his business, lost his money. We came penniless. Now I am a rich man. My riches are my family. We are going to a new home in two months. We'll have good fortune, as my father used to say, 'Change your place and you change your luck.' Let's all drink to our new home."

Charles H. Freundlich

LOUIS' OPTIMISM was most prophetic, and the family loved and relished their new apartment in the West Bronx. They made new friends, and lived comfortably on his Social Security. He attended a small *shtiebel* like his previous one. Shortly thereafter, the boys married and moved away, as Gittel had anticipated.

VYSE AVENUE was devastated in the whirlwind of urban decay throughout the East Bronx. The once attractive and desirable apartment buildings were abandoned by landlords; and torched by addicts, who were stealing the metal plumbing. Only a few brownstones remained. Sol took his young son to visit his apartment building, a short time before it was demolished. It was a street that could have personified Hiroshima. Urban renewal witnessed some new construction on Vyse Avenue, mostly, town houses.

Hardly an echo remains of the many immigrants, Jewish, Italian, Polish, and Irish - new Americans, with passionate hopes for their children and a brighter future. Their children's exuberant and ebullient life - when Stickball was predominant - the candy store was the hub of social life - and the streets were playgrounds - is recollected mostly by sentimental, former Bronxites.

ABOUT THE AUTHOR

CHARLES H. FREUNDLICH was born and raised in New York City, graduated from Talmudical Academy High School, Brooklyn College, B.A., and Yeshiva University's Bernard Revel Graduate School, where he received an M.A. and Doctor of Hebrew Literature. He studied at various yeshivas in New York and at Yeshivat Mercaz HaRav in Jerusalem, where he was ordained by the Chief Rabbi.

He served pulpits in Johnstown, Norfolk, Toronto, The Bronx, and Delray Beach and authored, *Peretz Smolenskin: His Life and Thought*, a study of Jewish nationalism. His numerous writings appeared in The Jewish Press.

He is married to Deborah (Schmerler), has four children, five grandchildren, and makes his home in Boca Raton, Florida.

Charles H. Freundlich

15775490R00152

Made in the USA
San Bernardino, CA
06 October 2014